"Don't ask any questions!" the driver growled.

"Nothing will happen to you if you cooperate." He slid the limousine's glass partition shut with a snap.

Catherine shrank back in her seat, her face as pale as her lace veil. Her mind spun with the shocking realization— she was being kidnapped on her wedding day!

Her first impulse was to throw herself out of the speeding vehicle. But by the time she gathered up her voluminous satin skirts, the driver would surely guess her intentions. The full, hindersome folds of her wedding gown, spread so carefully around her, formed an effective exquisite trap....

Other

MYSTIQUE BOOKS

by SUZANNE CLAUSSE

Bride's Ransom

by SUZANNE CLAUSSE

MYSTIQUE BOOKS

TORONTO·LONDON·NEW YORK
HAMBURG·AMSTERDAM·STOCKHOLM

BRIDE'S RANSOM / first published July 1980

Copyright © 1980 by Worldwide Library.
Copyright © MCMLXV by Librairie Jules Tallandier, as
OMBRE CHERIE.
Philippine copyright 1980. Australian copyright 1980.
ISBN 0-373-50085-8

Chapter 1

The reflection in the tall, oval mirror showed Catherine an image of herself she would never have believed possible a scant six months before. Yet there she stood, looking a little like she was going to a costume party— except for the fact that the couturiere and her assistant were still hovering around her, tucking and pinning last-minute alterations.

The gown, liberally trimmed with lace, was of ivory satin; against her naturally tawny skin the color made her dark blue eyes all the more startling. Her curly brown hair had been combed up for the occasion, exposing her long, graceful neck, and she thought that the whole effect made her look older than her twenty-two years. The traditional style of the gown gave her a rather proud, noble look, one that she wasn't used to and one that she found disconcerting. *Perhaps it's just as well,* she told herself silently. Mathias, after all, was ten years older than she was, and she didn't want to look like his kid sister on the day they were married.

Married. Catherine turned the word over in her mind and couldn't help giving an amused smile. Mrs. Ma-

thias Brunton. *Do you, Catherine Moreau, take this man
to be your lawfully wedded husband?*

Would she? Was she doing the right thing? It had
been such a whirlwind courtship that Catherine really
hadn't had much time to think about it. Mathias was
handsome, amusing and sociable, and already he was
indispensable to her father in his business. He seemed
to know everyone worth knowing in Paris, and was
clearly very much in love with her. But did she really
love him? Enough to marry him, to spend the rest of
her life with him? After all, she'd only met him last
March; now, the first week in September, she was marrying him.

During rehearsals at the church, it had felt very right;
she hadn't had a single doubt. But now that it was her
actual wedding day, she wasn't so sure anymore. She
knew better than to say anything, however. Her father
would just say she was suffering from bride's jitters,
while dear old Josephine would probably burst into
tears and plead with her not to marry Mathias unless
she could do so without any reservations.

"Turn to your left, please," the couturiere said,
standing back a little. "That's far enough, dear."

It was probably too late to change her mind anyway,
Catherine thought, turning away from the mirror and
staring out the window. They had taken over the master bedroom, which her father had let her use on this
special occasion. Her own bedroom, while more than
adequate for her normal needs, was too small to comfortably hold three women and a wedding gown.

"Another quarter turn, dear. That's it."

Mindlessly Catherine did as she was told, but she
wished the woman would stop calling her "dear." She
couldn't abide endearments from people she didn't

really know, feeling that they were superficial and dishonest. Even as a young girl Catherine had resented fawning people, which was probably why she'd never been able to feel comfortable around her cousin Roberta. Actually, Roberta was her uncle's widow, but ever since Catherine's own mother had died, her father had come to rely more and more upon Roberta to act in her place when an occasion required it. It had been at her father's insistence that Roberta had become her matron of honor, and Catherine was certain that during the wedding and the reception the sharp woman would try to take over the privileges of the mother of the bride.

For the thousandth time during the past few weeks Catherine wished her mother were still alive. She had always missed her terribly, but today, on her wedding day, the recognition of her loss was especially painful. She'd been only eleven when her mother died. Catherine remembered that she had been at boarding school when her father had paid her a special midsemester visit. She could still recall the shock she had felt at his words, the feeling of emptiness, as if everything important in her world had suddenly vanished.

Catherine had loved her mother deeply. Strangely enough, however, her memories of the woman were not so much physical ones as they were emotional. She knew her mother had had a warm, infectious laugh; that she loved playing tennis and swimming, going places and doing things. She had often hugged Catherine, and in other ways had reminded her how much she cared, and how happy she was to have her for a daughter. But try as she might, Catherine couldn't remember what the woman looked like. There were no photographs of her in the house, for when she had come home from school that week, unable to concentrate on anything except her grief, her father had already removed them. He had even taken down the portrait of her that used to hang in his study—it was almost as if, for him, Edith Moreau had never existed. He never voluntarily spoke her name, and Catherine, despite her youth, soon realized that he didn't want to talk about his wife again.

Josephine had been the only outlet for Catherine's grief. The wizened old woman, who had once been Mr. Moreau's nanny, had also raised Catherine. In the years since Mrs. Moreau's death, Josephine had continued to mother the girl with loving gentleness. Sometimes, however, Catherine thought she detected a troubled, wistful gaze in Josephine's brown eyes whenever the woman looked at her.

As if reading her mind, Josephine entered the bedroom at that moment and gasped in surprise. Her bony, arthritic fingers twisted together as tears welled up in her eyes. "You're the living image of your mother," she said, shaking her head.

Catherine turned as best she could, a delighted smile on her mouth. "Am I? Am I really, Josephine?"

Josephine nodded, her dark eyes revealing sadness as well as pleasure. "If only she were here today, how proud she'd be to see you!"

"Oh, Josephine," Catherine began, automatically moving toward the woman with her arms outstretched.

"Hold still, dear!"

"You have her eyes," Josephine added, raising her hand to indicate that Catherine should cooperate with the designer. "That same dark, smoky blue . . . almost slate. And her coloring, too."

"I'm so glad," Catherine replied, her eyes misting.

"You know, child, it might upset your father a little, seeing you. If he seems a little more gruff than usual, don't take it personally, all right?"

Catherine had to laugh. "More gruff than usual? He'd have to turn to granite!"

"Now, that's no way to talk about your father. I know he can be harsh and distant, but try to remember that he loved your mother very much. . . . His loss was every bit as great as yours."

"I know, I know! And then there's the business to run, and all his responsibilities. I certainly hope that Mathias isn't going to be like him! I want a husband and a loving father for our children . . . not a robot who thinks business is more important than life."

"That's something you won't find out about until later on, Catherine. During the courtship, most men have eyes and ears for nothing but their sweethearts. Later on they get back to business, earning a living, supporting their families, getting ahead. If you take an interest in Mathias's work, maybe you won't find yourself so shut out. That was something your mother never could do, however."

Catherine wondered if she'd be any different. It was difficult to find electronic components exciting or romantic, but she'd try. Transistors and conduits had never particularly stimulated her imagination, though they had certainly provided her with a very good lifestyle. She had always attended the very best schools, and on holidays she had gone with her father to first-class resorts. He liked to go fishing, enjoying the solitude the sport offered. As Catherine hadn't been able to share his enthusiasm, she had stayed near the resort, taking tennis lessons and joining the group activities offered—always under the careful eye of Josephine.

"There, dear, I think that should do it," the chic dress designer said, obviously pleased with herself. "You look stunning! Simply lovely!"

"It's a triumph," her assistant said, getting up from her knees with the pincushion in her hand.

A light rapping at the door interrupted their mutual congratulations, and Josephine went to open it. Mathias came into the room, looking particularly attractive in his cutaway.

"You shouldn't come in here!" Catherine said quickly, raising her hands to her face. "It's bad luck, Mathias!"

He shook his head with a smile. "With you as my wife, I won't need luck anymore. You're beautiful, Catherine."

"Don't go near her," the assistant cried. "You'll mess up her gown!"

Mathias stopped in his tracks, his firm mouth twisted in a somewhat patronizing smile. "I just wanted to tell you that your father's getting impatient, darling, and Roberta's practically beside herself. Are you almost ready?"

She gazed at the man who would soon be her husband. Mathias was quite tall, with a strong, masculine bearing. His deep tan showed his love of the sporting life. He particularly liked playing polo, and although it was a new world for Catherine, she had taken to his favorite sport instantly and had liked the people who followed the game. While not exactly jet set, polo was a rich man's game. It required a great deal of coordination and daring, and Mathias took great pride in the fact that he was a seven-goal man. Few players ever became that good.

"You're staring at me, darling," he said in his most tolerant voice.

"I'm sorry," Catherine said swiftly, wishing he wouldn't use that tone with her. That was the only time she was really aware of their age difference, and when he spoke like that she felt it was more like a reprimand from her father than a lover's tactful observation.

"Well, shall I tell the drivers to start the limousines?"

"Yes, I'll be right down," she answered.

"All right. Maybe Roberta and I should go on ahead to the church, then. She and I can put our guests at ease until the ceremony begins." He turned toward the door, then glanced back at her again. "The next time I see you, darling, we'll be getting married. Are you frightened?"

"Yes. Are you?"

"No, but that's because I'm sure of my love for you."

"Oh, Mathias, as if I wasn't sure of mine for you!"

He nodded sagely. "Don't worry about it, darling. I've loved you for a very long time, and I've had more of a chance to let the emotion grow and deepen." He smiled, blew her a kiss, then left the room.

Catherine glanced at Josephine and saw a covert look of disapproval on her lined face. "Will I be happy with him?" she asked.

"I hope so, child . . . I hope so."

"Then I suppose I may as well go downstairs before dad starts to bellow."

"Be careful with your gown," the designer warned.

Catherine held her head erect and moved cautiously to the door. The assistant placed herself ahead of Catherine at the top of the stairs, Josephine followed slowly behind, and the couturiere hovered next to Catherine, still fussing with the folds of her wedding dress. She felt as if she were surrounded by bodyguards. *My body-guards*, Catherine thought with a smile. Slowly they descended the broad staircase and entered the large living room where Mr. Moreau was waiting. He turned and, from beneath dark, thick-set brows, his steel-gray eyes examined the group. Catherine waited for him to say something—anything!

He took out his pocket watch, snapped open the lid, then closed it and returned the watch to his pocket. "It's taken nearly two hours for you to get dressed," he said somberly.

"But aren't you pleased, Mr. Moreau? Isn't she divine?"

Her father glanced at the dress designer, then nodded. "You've done very well, Miss Hagstrom. The dress is beautiful."

Catherine could feel herself tensing, but Josephine stepped closer, as if to remind her to be patient. Why was it so difficult for the man to say something nice to her? If it was because she looked so much like her mother, his attitude was very unfair; Catherine had no control over what she looked like! And it wasn't a question of his being too reserved to pay compliments; he could when he wanted to. If he could tell the designer that the dress was beautiful, why couldn't he say something nice to Catherine as well? What cosmic catastrophe did he fear would fall upon them if he said something encouraging, even flattering, to her? As she had so often in the past, Catherine wondered if the man loved her at all. He had done his duty toward her, had fed and clothed and educated her, but there was a lot more to parenthood than just that.

"We'd better get going, Catherine," Mr. Moreau was

saying. "You don't want to be late for your own wedding."

She was about to retort that she was not usually late for anything, but the warning look in Josephine's eyes stopped her. "Father," she said instead, in as calm a tone as she could, "aren't you pleased by my marriage? Mathias was your choice of husband for me. . . . Have you changed your mind?"

"No, of course not. What a silly question, Catherine."

"You don't seem very happy, though. You're acting as if we're going to attend a board meeting together, not my wedding."

"I suppose I've been preoccupied lately," he said, his cold gray eyes assessing her with a little more warmth. "I am very glad you decided to accept my advice and marry Mathias. He's a fine young man with a brilliant future ahead of him. One day he may even own Moreau Electronics, instead of just being our best account executive."

"But that's business, father. What does your heart tell you about my wedding?"

"My heart? I don't make decisions based on emotionalism, Catherine. That would be foolish."

Catherine sighed, knowing that she had once again reached an impasse with her father. He hadn't said a word about wanting her to be happy, nor had he even offered her his best wishes for her future. For a fleeting second Catherine wanted to hug her father, to be near him. But she knew he would stiffen as he always did. Besides, there were the two ladies from the dress designing firm as well. As usual, she had to put aside her own needs and wishes so that she wouldn't embarrass this man who had known her all her life.

It suddenly occurred to Catherine how little she really knew about life, about emotions and love. She had had so little love herself since her mother had died. Was she marrying Mathias to get away from her father's aloofness, she wondered? But no, she could have moved out when she'd finished college; she hadn't been forced to live in their huge home. It was clear that she couldn't speak to her father about love and marriage. Would she be able to talk to Mathias about her innermost feelings, or would he, too, be disinterested? Why hadn't she ever noticed before that Mathias and she seldom talked about their private thoughts? She wasn't really worried, however. Mathias was so totally different from her father that Catherine was sure he would listen to her seriously if the need ever arose. *More bride's jitters*, she thought to herself.

"Shall we go?" she asked.

"Yes," her father replied.

Just as they reached the foyer, the telephone rang. "Damn," Mr. Moreau said under his breath, moving toward his study. "You go ahead, Catherine. Josephine and I will come along later."

"Why can't Josephine come with me now?" Catherine asked.

"I don't have time to argue, Catherine!" he replied, frowning as he entered his den.

"Go along, child," Josephine urged gently. "We'll join you at the church in a few minutes."

"But we won't arrive together! I'll feel awful riding in that big limousine by myself!"

"Now, now, it's a short drive."

Disappointed, Catherine left the three-storied Tudor house and carefully walked down the front steps. A uniformed chauffeur, who had been leaning against the gleaming fender of the large black car, stood at attention when he saw her, and then opened the rear door for her.

She climbed in, carefully arranging her full skirt around her and feeling terribly sorry for herself. As a result, she hardly paid any attention as the driver got behind the wheel. He started the engine, then slowly pulled out of the driveway. Catherine, looking back at the house, felt her heart ache briefly for all the loving memories it should have held for her . . . but didn't. As a result, she didn't notice the chauffeur press a button that automatically locked all four doors.

When they reached the street, the driver stepped on the gas pedal. Soon they were moving almost too quickly for a residential area. When they arrived at the first major intersection, the chauffeur turned left, which Catherine noticed was the opposite direction from the church. Distracted from her morose thoughts at last, she leaned forward and rapped on the glass partition.

"Driver," she called. He slid the panel open and leaned his head back as if to hear her better. "Yes, miss?"

"You're going the wrong way. You should've turned . . ."

Just then a man in a dark blue sweater loomed up from the floor on the passenger side of the front seat. His thin face was tight and expressionless. "We've taken the best route for where we want to go," he said smoothly.

"Who . . .?"

"Don't ask any questions, Miss Moreau. I won't answer them. I suggest you make no effort to escape or to hinder us. The doors are locked and are controlled from the dashboard. If you cooperate nothing will happen to you."

"But where are you . . .?"

"No questions!" His voice was harsh and his dark eyes flashed a warning before he turned away. "You're being kidnapped, but you'll be all right as long as you do what we say!"

Catherine shrank back in the seat, her face white with fear and disbelief. Who were these thugs, her mind cried out. What did they want? Judging from the looks of the second man, Catherine didn't doubt for a moment that he would harm her if he was provoked.

The thin-faced man slid the partition closed again and seated himself with his back against the door, so that he could still watch her.

"My God, my God!" Catherine whispered to herself, her lips numb with fear.

Chapter 2

It had all begun in March when Catherine had completed her studies at the Academy of Graphic and Photographic Arts. She'd been given her certificate midterm, along with a few other students who had skipped the summer vacation to continue their courses.

Mr. Moreau had originally wanted his daughter to study business administration at university, but after the first semester she had rebelled. Catherine had always loved photography, even as a young girl, and she decided to pursue it as a career.

"It's no job for a woman," her father had protested. "You meet only the seamier types of men, the kind who probably peddle objectionable postcards in Pigalle!"

"Oh, father, you're being hopelessly old-fashioned," she had said, striving to keep her tone jocular and light. "It's a highly respected profession nowadays, and there are all types of photography. There's industrial photography, marine, and portraiture, still life, reportage . . . I could go on and on. It's an exciting and creative field, and if one is successful, a very well-paid occupation."

"You've hit the nail on the head, Catherine: *if* you're successful! You might as well be an actress! No, I do not approve. I want you to work in the factory with me. I am not going to live forever, you know, and as I don't have a son, you're going to have to know about the business. I expect you to respect my wishes in this matter, get a degree in business administration, then work at Moreau Electronics. Is that clear?"

"Father, it's very clear," she'd said quietly, not wanting to hurt his feelings, "but it's *my* life we're discussing. For one thing, you're still practically a young man by today's standards. Many men of fifty are in as good shape as they were when they were twenty . . . you've got lots of life ahead of you!"

"Are you defying me, Catherine? Is ingratitude part of the modern generation's attitude?" His tone had been shocked as well as severe.

Catherine had looked down, trying to find the right words she needed. She had made a special trip home for the weekend, having decided to tell her father that she hated her studies in business, and that she would really prefer to learn photography. Never before in her life had she stood up to him, and it was taking all the courage she could muster; but Catherine knew that if she didn't stand up to him now, she would be under his thumb forever. Finally, she lifted her dark blue eyes and faced him squarely. "I don't mean any disrespect, father . . . please believe that. But I think there are two factors you should consider before closing your mind to this discussion."

He had turned his back on her, ostensibly to look out his den window; she knew from long experience, however, that her father simply didn't like looking into her eyes. Taking a deep breath, she went on before he could terminate the discussion. "If you want me to be happy, you have to understand that I hate my classes. Even more importantly, wouldn't you prefer to see me successful at my chosen field, rather than miserable in the business you've built up? You know better than I do that an unhappy employee isn't worth anything to a company."

"In other words," he'd said tightly, "you intend to do as you wish, regardless of how I feel."

It's now or never, she'd thought, staring at the back of his gray head. "I'd like to have your approval, father, which is why I wanted to discuss my future with you today. But, in truth, if you withhold your consent . . . then, yes, I intend to do it anyway."

"And how will you pay for your classes? What if I cut off your tuition expenses, your allowance, and refuse to pay for your clothes?"

Catherine had swallowed hard, already prepared for that argument. "Then I shall have to apply for a scholarship and get a job. It'll take me longer to complete my studies, but I'll manage."

He'd turned slowly and they had stood facing each other silently. Catherine stood with her shoulders back, her face serious but not defiantly hostile.

"You're determined, then."

"Yes, sir."

Her father moved toward his mammoth mahogany desk and sat down heavily. He picked up the sterling silver letter opener she had given him for Christmas one year and tapped the point of it on the blotter in front of him. After deliberating for a few moments, he again looked up at her. "You have me in a very delicate position, Catherine. While I'm pleased to see you showing some independence, I'm very disappointed by your decision."

"I've tried to do what you wanted, father, but it just isn't working out."

"Would you consider a compromise?"

Catherine could hardly believe her ears. It was the first time in her life that her father had treated her as an equal. "Of course," she'd said.

"I'll continue to support you for one year while you study photography. At the end of that year, I'll arrange to speak with your teachers and counselors. If they fail to convince me of your superior—outstandingly so, Catherine—abilities in your pursuit, then you'll drop out and go back to the Sorbonne. I think you'll agree that what I'm asking is quite fair."

It wasn't at all fair and Catherine knew it. Few students showed any marked excellence during their first year in school, particularly in such a creative field. However, she instinctively realized she had pushed her father as far as he would bend. She'd simply have to work much harder than most students in order to avoid a breach with her father.

"All right, I agree," she replied seriously.

"Then I believe we can consider this conversation closed, Catherine."

"Yes, sir," she'd said, desperately trying to hold back her triumphant smile as she moved toward the door. She couldn't wait to tell Josephine what had transpired.

"Oh, Catherine, one more thing," Mr. Moreau called.

"Sir?"

"You're only eighteen, but I know what it cost you to come here this afternoon. You and I have never been close. However, I want you to know that I appreciate your consulting with me. It was merely a courtesy, perhaps, but it does show that you respect your father. I'm glad of that."

Not knowing what to say in response, she had nodded her head and escaped as quickly as she could. But once outside his den, tears of pain and happiness had welled up in her eyes. Her father had not only treated her as an adult, he had even said something nice to her!

That had been four years ago, and since that time she had more than proven herself. She had sold some of her photographs to newspapers and had even done some fashion work for a couple of smaller Paris magazines. It wasn't much, but Catherine felt that it was a start.

By the end of her last term at school, however, all the hard work she had put in seemed to have taken its toll. She felt tired at the time and never had any energy. After a while she seemed to be running a fever, and she constantly had a sore throat. Josephine, finding out about her condition, had insisted she see a physician, who diagnosed her condition as mononucleosis. The disease was commonplace among college students, she was told, and only complete rest would improve her condition.

It was then, in March, that Catherine had come home to recuperate, realizing that she would have to leave job-hunting for when she felt better. Josephine, naturally, hovered over her constantly, bringing her steaming mugs of broth to build up her strength and cool compresses for her fever. For the first week or ten days, Catherine was content to stay in bed, but after she had read every book she could find, boredom began to take over.

When she was feeling a little stronger she amused herself by seeing how many different ways she could photograph her own room and its contents. She set her camera on a tripod and studied every item in the room as if she had never seen it before. Was a lamp a simple source of light, or did it bring balance and juxtaposition to a corner of her room? Could it look like something else at a new angle? Nothing escaped her lens. A photo of a bureau was mundane, but when she framed the shot so that only one knob appeared against the grain of the wood, the end result was a study in contrast and form.

Because the Moreau house, naturally enough, didn't have a darkroom—nor was Catherine well enough to use it if she had had access to one—she sent her film out to a professional lab to be developed. When the contact sheets came back to her, she would pore over them with a magnifying glass and a grease pencil, indicating which shots she wanted enlarged and how she wanted them cropped.

On one such afternoon, Josephine had come to her room with a suspicious glint in her dark eyes. "Why aren't you in bed?" she demanded.

Catherine smiled, not even looking up from the proof sheets in front of her. "I'm sitting down, Josephine. That's resting, too."

"It's not the same as being in bed," the old woman had argued firmly. "What are you doing, anyway?"

"Here." Catherine had handed the glass to Josephine. "Look for yourself. What do you see?"

Josephine peered over her glasses. "A lot of photos of your bureau. You didn't even get the whole thing in the picture!"

"What do you think this is?" Catherine then asked, handing her another proof sheet with a laugh.

"I don't know," Josephine had replied with a shrug. "But if it's something in this room, give the thing to me and I'll throw it away."

"Josephine," Catherine laughed, "it's my lamp, the one over there."

The woman gave her back the sheet with a snort. "Well, if you know what's good for you, you'll never let your father see these! He'll think he's thrown away his money on your education, and there'll be the devil to pay, that's for sure!"

Catherine had hugged Josephine fondly. "I'm surrounded by blind people," she had groaned.

"I've got better eyesight than you do," Josephine remarked. "At least when I take a picture of something, it looks like what it should! Now, back into bed with you!"

"Now?"

"Now!"

Catherine did as she was told, knowing it was useless to argue. As the older woman pulled the comforter up around her chin, she went on, "Will father be home for supper tonight?"

"As far as I know. Why?"

"Because I want to ask him something."

Josephine's eyebrows rose quizzically. "I suppose you've decided to become a tightrope walker."

"No, silly. I want him to let me do some photography for this year's annual report. There are never any pictures in those awful brochures, and I bet many of the stockholders have no idea what an electronics factory looks like. It could be fun for them to find out, don't you think? And photos would make the report infinitely more attractive."

"I wouldn't know. Now you get some sleep."

"Josephine?"

"Hmm?"

"Why are there no pictures of my mother in the house?"

The woman paused near the doorway. "You know the answer to that. They were all put away after she . . . she died."

"And her portrait? There used to be a portrait of her, I'm sure!" Catherine started to sit up in bed, but when Josephine glared at her she snuggled down again.

The woman got a faraway look in her eyes. "It's around somewhere," she said, coming back to the side of the bed and plumping the pillows. "In the attic, I suspect. I don't know. Maybe he gave it away."

"I hope not," Catherine had said, stifling a yawn. "It would mean a great deal to me if I could see what she looked like."

"Look in the mirror, then," Josephine said simply. "Now, enough of this. It's time for your nap. You're looking too pale for my liking."

"If it's a nice day tomorrow, could I sit outside in the garden?"

"If it's warm enough." She placed her gnarled hand on her patient's forehead, then nodded to herself.

"I love you, Josephine," Catherine murmured.

The woman's eyes softened and a sweet-sad smile came to her lips. "I love you, too, child. Go to sleep now."

THE FOLLOWING DAY was typically brisk for March, but the sun was out and Catherine managed to talk Josephine into letting her sit out on the terrace. St. Cloud was one of the better residential areas outside of Paris proper, and the Moreaus' home had an unusually large backyard. The flower beds were still in their winter dormancy, but soon the crocuses and daffodils would be coming up, followed by tulips and violets. It was a pleasant yard, but unimaginative, and Catherine had often longed for a break from the carefully planned symmetry of its walks and hedges. The trees were planted evenly, the hedges trimmed to precisely the same height, and the low wall enclosing the yard was uniformly perfect to the point of dullness. But at least out there she could breathe the fresh air and feel the sun on her face and hair.

Catherine wondered if this garden had looked the same when her mother had been alive, and seriously doubted it. She had always presumed that she had got her lively imagination from her mother, since both her father and Josephine were so practical about everything. For a moment, she tried to envision the yard as it had looked during her childhood, but her memory refused to cooperate.

The sudden noise of a chain saw reached her ears and she glanced over at the yard next door in annoyance. A man was straddling a thick branch of one of the trees, with the awkward machine propped up in front of him as he sawed the limb next to him. The grating noise seemed to whine on endlessly, then it stopped. She watched as the man leaned forward and pushed down on the edge of the branch, until a creaking, almost wrenching sound began and she heard the man say, "Dammit—here we go!"

As if in slow motion, the branch begin to break away from the trunk of the tree, and seconds later, branch and man fell to the ground out of sight. Frantically she tried to get out of her chair, but Josephine had wrapped her too snugly and she was virtually a prisoner under the blankets. "Are you all right?" she finally called in desperation.

She waited for him to reply, but there was no answer. "Hello over there," she called again. "Are you okay?"

A moment later she saw the man pull himself up to his feet with the aid of the wall. Between gasps of breath he managed to say, "I'm—okay. Knocked—the—wind out—of me."

He was wearing jeans and, despite the time of year, only a light cotton T-shirt. Catherine could see that he was a broad-shouldered fellow, with a well developed chest and a trim waistline. His hair was dark brown, almost black, and he wore it collar length. His arms were still resting on the low wall, when he finally looked up at her. "I think I'll live," he said, grinning sheepishly.

"That was a nasty fall," she said. "Are you certain you didn't break anything?"

He felt his ribs with one hand, and she couldn't help noticing how muscular his bare arms were. He seemed like an unusual type of person to be a gardener; but then, so many young men were rebelling against the corporate world these days, preferring to do physical labor than sit at a desk.

"Nope, everything seems intact." He held his hands up as if to show her that he was unarmed. "May I come over?"

"I guess so, if you like," she answered, uncertain of what to say but unable to think of any reason why he shouldn't.

When he reached the terrace, she saw that he had

large, soft brown eyes, with black lashes fringing them. Though their color wasn't particularly arresting, they were wide set and seemed to dominate his angular face. A very slight bump along the bridge of his otherwise straight nose told her that he must have broken it at one time or another. His mouth was wide, with wrinkles at the corners from laughing. He was actually a very handsome young man, and Catherine couldn't help wondering again why he didn't have better job somewhere. She could tell by his long legs and fine features that he was of sensitive stock, which aroused her curiosity all the more.

He sat down on the wrought-iron chair opposite hers and examined her with unconcealed candor. "You look as if you're ready to sink with the *Titanic*," he said, laughing.

She had to laugh with him, enjoying the picture in her mind. "I do feel a bit as if I've been strapped to a deck chair."

"Obviously, we can't shake hands," he said, still smiling. "You don't remember me, do you?"

"Have we met?" She tried to think of where she might have encountered him, but doubted that she'd ever forget such a good-looking fellow.

"I'm Michael—Michael Andrews, your neighbor."

"Michael! Scrawny, pinching, nosy Michael? The scourge of the block?"

"The same," he replied, grinning. "I wouldn't have recognized you either, except for the color of your eyes. I've never forgotten how unusual they are."

"B-but I thought . . . after the death of your parents . . . that . . . ."

"Yes, the house was boarded up for a number of years. I've been away a great deal, and anyway, I felt that it was too big a place for me to rattle around in all alone. But my paper recently transferred me to the Paris office, so I thought I'd move back in."

"Wait a minute," Catherine pleaded good-naturedly. "That's a lot to get straight. The last time I saw you, I guess I was about fourteen."

"That sounds right. I must have been sixteen or so. When my folks died, I was packed off to live with my aunt and uncle in America. I finished my education there, got a job with a New York newspaper and—"

Catherine laughed, and for some reason it felt exceptionally good, as if she hadn't found anything to laugh at in a very long time. "But Michael, back up a second! You make it all sound as if you'd just run to the drugstore for a pack of cigarettes! You've been to America . . . you're working for a New York newspaper . . . ."

"No, no," he corrected her. "I used to work for a paper in New York, but that was a while back. Since then I've been a foreign correspondent for *Paris Match* magazine, I worked for the international edition of the *Herald-Tribune*, and for the last year and a half I've been with *L'Express*. It's really very simple."

"If I'd been leading your life, maybe," Catherine chuckled. "But to me it all sounds very complicated and glamorous!"

"You'll have to forgive me," Michael said. "I often have to phone in my news stories, so I've learned to pack in a lot of pertinent information into quick sentences. Then some poor bloke tied to a desk fills in all the adjectives and makes it sound good." He shivered briefly. "It's pretty chilly out here if you're not moving around. Speaking of which, why are you all bundled up like that?"

Catherine gave an exaggerated sigh. "I've been sick and Josephine wouldn't let me come outside unless I promised to keep warm."

"Do you have a blanket to spare?"

"I must have dozens! Please, take the top one if you can get it off of me."

He leaned over and gently pried loose the corners of the neatly tucked-in coverlet, then removed it and threw it around his shoulders. "What we need is a fire in a trash can—then we could pretend we were hoboes, waiting to catch the next freight train."

"Aren't we supposed to have a can of beans or something?"

"A bottle of cheap wine is more like it."

A brief silence fell between them, but it was a comfortable one. "Do you mind if I smoke?" Michael asked finally, pulling a pack of cigarettes out of his hip pocket.

"No, go ahead. When did you move back into the house?" she asked.

"Last week. I've been trying to get it cleaned up by myself, but I'm about to give in and hire a team to come over to do it. Housework has never been one of my strong points."

Catherine smiled, secretly admitting that it wasn't her favorite activity either. "Are you planning to live here permanently now?"

"Maybe. A lot depends on my job. I'd like to, I think. But what about you? What have you been doing these past years?"

She shrugged. "School—that's about it. I had just graduated when I came down with mono. Nothing as exciting as your accomplishments."

"You've certainly blossomed into a very lovely young woman, Catherine."

Pleased at the compliment, she smiled at him. "Then why were you always so rotten to me when we were kids?"

"C'mon, we hardly saw each other, you know that. Besides, all teenage boys are mean to girls they find attractive. It's par for the course."

"I didn't know you were atttracted to me. I thought you hated me!"

"Just goes to prove that you never know what's going on in a man's heart. But I'll try to make up for that now that we're grown-up. I promise not to pinch you, make faces, or try to trip you as you go by."

"I suppose I'll find a measure of comfort in that," she said, feeling very glad to renew her acquaintance with Michael. He had an easy, gracious way about him, and a warm glow in his eyes. She liked him, and it was rare for Catherine to like someone the first time they met.

Chapter 3

That evening, while Catherine and Mr. Moreau were having coffee after supper, she told him about getting reacquainted with their handsome neighbor. Mr. Moreau, as usual, had spent most of the meal discussing what was going on at the factory, more to fill up the silence than because Catherine was really interested.

"Did young Andrews say why he's moved back to St. Cloud?" Her father took the sugar bowl as she handed it to him.

"Well, we didn't really have a chance to talk that much. He's been so busy with his career that . . . ."

"What does he do? His father, of course, was very respected in the diplomatic service. Nice fellow. I was most distressed to learn of Mr. and Mrs. Andrews's death. Shocking, really."

"Weren't they killed in an auto accident or something?" Catherine asked, passing the cream and inspecting the Limoges plate, which was piled high with assorted cookies.

"No, they were caught in the cross fire of a terrorist raid in Lebanon. Mr. Andrews had served there for a number of years, but they were back there on vacation when it happened."

"How awful!"

Mr. Moreau nodded absently. "But you still haven't told me what Michael does for a living."

"He's a newspaper reporter," she answered, then told him about the various places Michael had worked and lived.

Mr. Moreau watched her quizzically as she talked, then said, "By the way, you remember Mathias Brunton, don't you?"

Catherine thought for a minute, then shook her head.

"You met him a couple of times when you were much younger. Mathias came to work for me, oh, I'd say about six years ago. He's a dedicated employee and has done very well, working his way up practically from the bottom."

"Is he rather tall and blond?"

"That's right. He's now our account executive, and he's virtually indispensable to Moreau Electronics. Mathias will be coming here all week to help me prepare the annual stockholders' report, starting tomorrow. He'll come for supper, and afterward we'll work in my study.

She smiled, trying to think of something appropriate to say. "It'll be nice to see him again. I'll ask Mrs. Campbell to prepare something special. Maybe a nice roast beef . . . ."

"No, beef is too hard on the digestion. Chicken or fish would be better, I think."

Catherine leaned back in her chair, toying with the handle on her coffee cup. "Father, I'd like to suggest something."

"Yes?"

"How about illustrating this year's report with photographs of the factory and some of the key personnel?"

"What on earth for? Stockholders are interested in profit and loss. They don't care how their dividends are made as long as they get their money on time."

"But I think they should be interested, father," she said, leaning forward excitedly. "Think of the favorable public relations the factory would get if the stockholders knew it was something more than a column of figures. The personal touch! Showing people at their jobs, the sparks of a welding machine symbolically showing that Moreau Electronics is part of the future of France . . . that sort of thing!"

"Humph!" was Mr. Moreau's only reply.

"Please think about it, father, won't you? Many big corporations have pictures in their stock reports . . . why shouldn't we? They're obviously not interested in squandering their assets, so the photographs must seem worthwhile to their own management boards. If nothing else, it must at least give people a sense of satisfaction to be reminded that their investment is providing jobs, keeping people off the unemployment lists."

Mr. Moreau sipped his coffee, then dabbed at his salt-and-pepper mustache with his napkin. "How much more expensive would it be?" he asked slowly, his gray eyes unreadable.

"Generally you use a very porous paper for your reports. Right off the bat we'd have to use better paper, suitable for reproduction. An added expense would be using four-color photos instead of black-and-white, but of course that would make the report that much more attractive."

Her father stirred his coffee, frowning. "Perhaps big corporations illustrate their reports as a tax write-off. I'm afraid, Catherine, that your proposal could be unnecessarily expensive for us."

She smiled impishly. "But think of how much you'd save on labor! My fees are modest, and I'd do the layout myself. . . ."

"Fees? You'd charge your own father?"

"No, of course not," she replied cheerfully. "But I'd charge the corporation. You always say that no one respects what they get free."

A hint of a smile crossed his lips for a moment. Catherine had never heard her father laugh, that she could remember, anyway, and she knew that a smile for him was what a guffaw was for others.

"I'm glad to see that you listen to me sometimes. But do you think you're able to handle the job? Are you well enough? We have to have it ready for the printer in six weeks."

"Six weeks! That's an eternity, father!"

"What about your illness?"

Catherine shook her head, as if the question was inane. "I'll concentrate on indoor shots first. Toward the end of April, when it's warmer, I'll get all the outdoor material. If I do everything Josephine says for the next week, that should make her happy, and me stronger."

When Mr. Moreau placed his napkin next to his plate and drew a panatela from his vest pocket, she got up and brought back an ashtray for him from the sideboard. Trying not to show her impatience, she watched him light the thin cigar, squinting his eyes in the smoke.

"I'm not going to say yes or no, Catherine. When Mathias is here tomorrow evening, take it up with him.

Frankly, I think it would be a waste of money, but if he thinks it's a good idea, then I'll go along with the majority opinion."

Outwardly Catherine retained her expression of polite interest, but inwardly she was elated. "I'll have to think of something delicious for Mrs. Campbell to make for dinner tomorrow, to put him in a good mood. I'm sure he'll agree that four-color will be much better looking than black-and-white."

"Not so quick, young lady. Mathias hasn't even heard your ideas, much less agreed to them!"

"He will, father," she said airily. "He will."

MATHIAS BRUNTON and Mr. Moreau arrived from the factory together the next evening, but in separate cars. When the gray sedan, which Catherine's father replaced every other year with the latest model, pulled into the driveway, it was followed by a bright yellow sports car. Catherine watched as a man about five-foot-eleven with sandy blond hair climbed out. He was wearing a dark tan corduroy suit and a very deep red knit tie. Even from a distance Catherine could tell that he was also wearing expensive leather loafers. It was obvious to her that he commanded a very substantial salary from her father, for though she didn't know very much about cars, she did know that sports cars could cost a pretty penny.

Mathias Brunton, who was carrying, a leather briefcase, paused to wait as his employer shut his car door with a precise, deliberate gesture. Suddenly, as if she was really seeing him for the first time, Catherine realized how old her father looked next to the younger man. The difference didn't appear so much in the lines of his face or in his gray hair as much as in his manner and movements. His steps seemed to require effort next to Mr. Brunton's easy stride; his shoulders, though straight, didn't exude the feeling of confidence of the younger man.

As the two men came up the walk, she continued comparing them. The young executive, gesturing and talking with her father, had a ready smile, as if he considered Mr. Moreau quite witty. His sandy-colored hair was just long enough to be stirred by the early evening breeze. Her father's gray hair, in contrast, was kept very short, in the same style she had sometimes noted in old movies. For a moment Catherine felt terribly sorry for her father, and she wondered what lonely thoughts traveled in his head in the stillness of the night. *Perhaps he should have remarried*, she thought, but instantly wiped the idea out of her mind. Though her memories of her mother were vague, she nonetheless felt an intense loyalty to her.

She went over to open the living-room door as the men climbed the steps, and then extended her hand to Mr. Brunton. "How very nice to see you again," she said warmly.

The young man's bluish green eyes studied her quickly. "You've grown into the beauty I knew you would, Catherine," he said, shaking her hand with a firm, brief grip.

A little uncomfortable under his admiring gaze, she leaned over and gave her father a kiss on the cheek. "Come in, please. It's chilly out here."

"And with the door open, we're heating the whole outdoors," Mr. Moreau said. "I see you do remember Mathias after all," he added, removing his overcoat and scarf and hanging them neatly in the hall closet.

"Yes, now that I see him again. I wasn't sure before,"

she answered. "But didn't you wear an overcoat, Mr. Brunton?"

"Please, let's not stand on ceremony," he said in a pleasant baritone. "Call me by my first name, Mathias, or you'll make me feel ancient. And I never wear a coat unless it's subzero—I find them too heavy and constricting."

She could readily believe it, for he had the look of a man who liked sports and activity. There was a masculine agility about him that belied his almost too handsome good looks. Leading the way into the living room, she went over to the fireplace and poked the logs with the fire tongs, being careful not to soil her long skirt. She had dressed carefully that evening in a full-length plaid wool skirt and a dark blue sweater. She knew perfectly well that the color of her sweater accented her slate-blue eyes, and that her outfit showed that the occasion was more than a casual one, yet not particularly formal. Catherine wanted Mathias Brunton to feel at ease and welcomed, so that he would be receptive to her ideas for the annual report.

"Do you really think we need a fire, Catherine?" her father asked as he went toward the liquor cart, which stood near the baby grand piano in the corner of the room.

"Oh, I thought it would be nice," she answered. "A fire always makes a room so much more cozy, don't you think, Mr. Bru—Mathias, that is."

"As much as candlelight at the dinner table," he answered, smiling a touch rakishly. He moved closer to the hearth and rubbed his hands together.

"What will you have, Mathias?" Mr. Moreau asked.

"A Scotch, if you have some," he answered, not taking his eyes away from Catherine. Then he addressed her. "I hear you've just graduated from school—photography, wasn't that your major?"

"Yes, though father gave me a hard time about it at first."

"She has some outlandish idea she wants to discuss with you, Mathias. I've already told her that I don't like it, but—"

"Oh, father, let's not talk about business so soon. We can do that later," she interrupted, smiling broadly. "I'm certain Mathias would far prefer to have a relaxing drink right now. Judging by the car you drive, I'm sure you put in a very hard day at the factory."

"Isn't she a beauty, though? She's got a front, water-cooled engine and a rear transaxle that gives her catlike stability on the road. I don't think there's a car on the market that can beat her performance."

"I daresay she's quite fast," Catherine said, not really comprehending the virtues Mathias had listed.

"I'll take you for a spin some day, if you like. She'll respond like a tiger even at 145 miles per hour!"

Catherine swallowed hard, then smiled. "That's a little faster than I'd care to experience," she replied. "Do you race?"

"No, I've dabbled in it occasionally, but polo is my game."

"Polo!" she repeated in amazement. "But where on earth do you play that around here?"

"There are a number of places, actually. Teams often rent the grounds at various riding academies, or we sometimes get permission from landowners to block off a polo field in a meadow. The sport's been getting a new wave of interest in France."

"I thought it was only for Americans and Englishmen," she answered, accepting a glass of white wine from her father as he joined them before the fire.

"Not really," Mathias said, nodding to Mr. Moreau as he removed his glass from the small enameled tray. "It's been an international sport for more than a hundred years. The Argentinians are fiendishly good at the game, for example. If I can get my handicap higher, I may even try out for a bit of international play this year."

"Your handicap?"

"Yes, you've heard people say that so-and-so is a three-goal man or a six-goal player—well, that's by way of showing your proficiency. An amateur is ranked at zero, and the better you get, the higher you're ranked. Until you reach ten, which is as high as anyone can go." He lifted his glass in a wordless toast, then continued. "Haven't you ever seen a game?"

"No," she admitted, sipping her wine.

"Then you must come watch me play!" Mathias gazed down at her. "Although it's not modest of me to say so, I'm very good at it, and it's a fast game, very much like soccer or hockey. You have to be a superb horseman to play it, naturally, or you risk getting killed. Polo is a game of skill and judgment, and as such it attracts a rather elite audience. The spectators are not only usually wealthy, but they're also knowledgeable about the game and ruthlessly demanding of the players."

"I suppose you have to have your own horse," she said, moving toward the dark brown couch and seating herself gracefully.

"I only wish I did," Mathias said. "Fortunately, a chum of mine breeds Arabians, and he's let me work with one of the mares whenever I have time. You

seldom have a chance to use the reins during the game,
so your mount has to know you very well and has to
respond to the pressure of your knees, or to how you're
sitting in the saddle. You need a very intelligent, quick
horse to win, but also one that won't spook easily."

Mr. Moreau lowered himself into a striped armchair
and swirled his whiskey around in his squat glass as
he said, "It's a miracle you haven't been trampled already, Mathias. I don't know what possesses you to
pursue these dangerous games." He took a swallow
from his drink, winced, then took another. "Frankly,
Catherine, it's his biggest fault. Anyone who continues
to challenge death will one day find out that the gaunt-
let has been accepted."

Mathias remained standing, leaning one elbow on
the mantel above the fireplace. "Well, sir, I spend five
days a week cooped up in an office—either mine or
a client's. I need the thrill of sports, the sensorial pleasure it provides."

"Sensorial?" Mr. Moreau's brows knit together as
if confused.

"Yes, sir. Think of it. The smell of leather and horse-
flesh; the sound of eight horses thundering across a
field and the resounding whack when mallet connects
with the ball; the feel of power beneath you as you
charge toward the goal, your arm swinging free until
it strikes the ball and sends it straight to your mark;
the cheers and the—"

"Okay, okay, that's enough," Mr. Moreau said,
shaking his head with a slight smile on his lips.

"Obviously," Catherine put in, "you love the game.
I'd love to watch you play some day. It would be great
fun."

"Wonderful! I'm playing this Sunday afternoon not

too far from here, as a matter of fact. Why don't I come by for you around ten-thirty? Would that be all right?"

For a split second, Catherine felt as if she were being pushed into going with him. Though she knew perfectly well she'd expressed interest, there was something in his manner that made her feel like she was being rushed into a decision. But then, she reminded herself, Mathias was an account executive, and success in getting new business often lay in closing a deal before the client could think twice about it. She'd learned that not only in school, but also in the years of listening to her father drone on about the electronics business.

"Would you like to come too, Pierre?" Mathias asked, turning to Mr. Moreau.

"No, no," the older man said, waving his left hand. "I've got better things to do than watch grown men on horseback chase a ball."

In a strange way, Catherine was almost sorry her father had refused to join them. There was something rather unsettling about Mathias Brunton, she was finding, although she couldn't quite put her finger on what it was.

Chapter 4

Fortunately, Sunday turned out to be a sunny day and unseasonably warm; otherwise, Catherine knew she would have had to do battle with Josephine in order to go out for the day. As it was, rather than risk the woman's ire, she bundled up in a green, cowl-neck sweater and a loosely tied matching cardigan over her favorite pair of beige wool slacks. And to guarantee she'd have no trouble with her former governess, Catherine donned a chic pair of oxblood boots. *If you're going to mix with the horsey crowd*, she thought, *it's best to look very countrified and genteel.*

Mathias arrived promptly at ten-thirty, and she was just dabbing on a bit of lipstick when Josephine came up to tell her that he was waiting for her.

"What do you think, Josephine? Do I pass muster?"

The old woman's lined face broke into a broad smile. "You'll do," she answered cryptically. "Now, I want you to wear a coat, Catherine, and take a lap robe."

"But Josephine, I'm already wearing two wool sweaters! I'll roast in anything else!"

"No, you won't. And unless you want me to insist that you go back to bed, you'll do as I say." The brown eyes brooked no nonsense. "You can just tell people that you've been ill. No one's going to laugh at you."

Catherine went over and put her arms about the woman's bony shoulders. "You're a terror, Josephine. Do you remember how you used to make me wear those awful union suits during the winter? Your argument was always the same—that no one could see what I was wearing under my clothes, so no one would laugh at me."

"You can make fun all you want to, Catherine, but I've raised a healthy child, and I'll not let you have a relapse just because you're a little older."

"All right, Josephine," she agreed, pulling back. "You win."

"I always do, Catherine . . . eventually. Now, be off with you and have a nice time. Don't forget you promised to come home before the evening chill sets in."

"I won't," Catherine said, kissing her on the cheek and dashing down the broad staircase to the main floor. "I'm ready," she called to Mathias, who stood in the foyer talking with her father.

"Great! Let's go," he answered. With a wave to Mr. Moreau, he escorted her to his waiting car. "I see you've brought your camera," he said, helping her into the passenger seat.

"It goes where I go," she answered, patting it fondly.

He grinned, then walked around to the driver's side and climbed in behind the wheel like the master of a ship. "It's a beautiful day for the game, and a perfect one for the drive."

"How far do we have to go?" she asked.

"Near Champeaux. We'll take the main highway, which will save time." He started up the engine, revved it a few times, then backed out of the driveway. "Do you think you'll be warm enough?" he asked with a smile, using his chin to gesture toward the coat and blanket she had folded in her arms.

"This is the only way I was allowed out of the house today," she answered, smiling back.

"Your father was telling me that you've been ill."

"I have been, but I'm not going to lug all this stuff around once we get to the match. I want to be free to move around and take some pictures. Speaking of which, I want to thank you for backing me up last Thursday. Father's given in about having photos in the annual report, and he's even going to let me put it together."

"I was just being selfish about all that, if you must know," Mathias said, adjusting his rearview mirror a fraction of an inch. "If you're going to be doing the layout, I'll have a chance to see more of you."

"You mean you don't really agree that it's a viable idea?" she asked, noticing that his hands were well manicured.

"Of course it is," he said, glancing at her briefly. "But if a man had made the same suggestion, I might not have sided with him so quickly. It's going to set us back a bit, and normally I don't encourage unnecessary expenditures."

Catherine shrugged. "It's tax-deductible, Mathias."

"Yes, and it'll look good in your portfolio, too," he teased.

She laughed. "Not really. I think most people will figure out that Catherine Moreau is somehow related to Moreau Electronics."

They chatted easily during the drive, and as the suburbs thinned, giving way to open country, Mathias began to open the throttle of his sports car. Catherine found it exhilarating to whiz past trees and pastures as if the world couldn't keep up with them. It felt wonderful to be out of the house, to see the cows and goats, the farmers with their wooden carts pulled by horses, and the small villages along the way. Perhaps some other time, she decided, she might come back to this area and spend a day taking pictures. She was enjoying the speed of the car, but normally she would have preferred a more leisurely drive.

When they arrived at the polo field, Mathias pulled up alongside a Rolls Royce and turned off the engine. Peering around, Catherine could see that quite a crowd had come to watch the game. Perhaps as many as seventy or a hundred people were milling about, chatting with one another as if they were old friends. To her right, eight superb-looking horses were being led in a large circle for the inspection of the crowd. They were already saddled and bridled, and occasionally one would arch its neck and whinny loudly. Closer to where the cars were parked and a respectable distance from the field itself, which had been loosely roped off, folding chairs had already been set up. A number of vans, obviously designed to transport horses, were hooked up to half-ton trucks, all bearing the names of breeders on their doors.

"Which horse is yours?" Catherine inquired as they drew nearer to the crowd.

"That one over there," he said, pointing. "The chestnut. Isn't she a beauty?"

"I don't know much about horses, but she's certainly quite magnificent looking. What's her name?"

"Windfire—a combination of her speed and her temperament. Come on, I'll introduce you."

"To a horse?" She laughed as he took her hand and

tugged her toward a group of people who were admiring the animals as they paraded by.

"Mathias! How *are* you, darling!" A tall, leggy woman wearing riding breeches had turned around and noticed Mathias. Catherine guessed from her accent as well as from her creamy complexion that she was English.

"Catherine? I'd like you to meet Lady Georgina Dickinson. Georgie, meet Catherine Moreau."

The tall woman looked down at Catherine as if she were of questionable suitability. "How do you do," she drawled, extending a limp hand.

"I'm pleased to meet you," Catherine said simply, getting rid of the handshake as quickly as possible.

Immediately linking her arm through Mathias's, Lady Dickinson said with a pout, "Is she the reason I haven't seen you at the club lately? I've *missed* you dreadfully."

"Actually, no," Mathias replied, winking at Catherine. "I've been working on our company's annual report."

"Nights, as well? But darling, that's absolutely *wicked* of you! You're the only good disco dancer in the entire club!"

"Yes, well, you've got to remember, Georgie, that I'm not independently wealthy. I do have to work, after all."

"I *do* wish you'd stop classing yourself with the proletariat, darling. It doesn't become you." Georgie turned and smiled feebly at Catherine. "I suppose you work, too, uh, what was your name again, dear?"

"I'm out of work at present," Catherine responded, already quite certain that she didn't like the woman at all.

"Catherine's a professional photographer, Georgie," Mathias chimed in. "Just like Princess Margaret's ex-husband," he added, a small gleam in his aquamarine eyes.

"I see," she commented. "How droll. Of course, Lord Snowdon doesn't *have* to work."

"One's employment is work only if you don't like what you're doing," Catherine said, keeping a pleasant smile on her face.

"I suppose so," the woman answered, gazing off over Catherine's head with a slightly bored expression.

"C'mon, Catherine," Mathias broke in. "I want you to meet Windfire. You'll excuse us, Georgie, won't you?" he added as he led Catherine away.

"Brrr!" Catherine said when they were out of earshot. "I'd certainly hate to sail in her waters!"

He laughed. "Georgie's not so bad. You just have to understand her, that's all."

"Is everyone here like that?"

"Not at all! Georgie just happens to have a small crush on me. She hates it when I have another date."

"But . . . isn't she married?"

"Of course," Mathias said casually. "Lord Dickinson is around somewhere, probably taking a nip from his flask and trying to entice a pretty young maiden to do the same."

Catherine decided to let the matter drop. While she herself heartily disapproved of extramarital flirtations, she admitted that it was really none of her business. It bothered her a little, however, that Mathias seemed to take the whole thing so lightly, as if that's what all married couples did.

They reached the circle of horses and Mathias went straight to Windfire and patted her neck. "Easy, girl, easy," he said in a gentle voice. He reached into the tight pocket of his riding breeches and pulled out a lump of sugar. "Here," he said, giving it to Catherine, "introduce yourself."

"Hello, Mathias," a robust man called as he came toward them. "Windfire's a little nervous today, I'm afraid."

"Hello, Harry," Mathias said, and introduced Catherine to the owner of the horse. "Do you think she's up for today's match?" he asked, an apprehensive look on his face.

"Of course. She's just a little skittish. Don't let them crowd her, if you can avoid it. But after a good run in the field, she should calm down soon enough." He turned to Catherine then, an approving beam on his ruddy face. "I must say, Mathias, your taste in women is every bit as good as it is in horses. She's lovely."

"Thank you," Catherine murmured, her cheeks pink.

Mathias put his arm about her shoulder and squeezed gently. "The boss's daughter, Harry, so be sure you're nice to her."

Harry glanced at his wristwatch, then back to Mathias. "It's about time for the match to start. Are you ready?"

"I just have to get my helmet and mallet out of the car. Be right back," he said, jogging off.

"Nice fellow, Mathias," the owner said, patting the horse's withers. "Known him long?"

"Only in a manner of speaking," she replied, noticing that Mathias was already heading back toward them. He'd removed his tweed jacket and pullover, revealing a navy blue T-shirt with The Wolves printed across the chest, and was carrying a dull white helmet with a short brim in front. He put it on as he approached them, then put the mallet's long handle under his arm while he pulled on a pair of riding gloves.

"Well? Do you like the uniform?"

"It's very . . . sporting," she said for lack of a better term, noting that three other men had removed their coats and were wearing the same shirts. "So your team is The Wolves," she said. "Who are your opponents?"

"They're over there," Harry announced. "They call themselves The Bennetts, after James Gordon Bennett, the fellow who made polo a popular sport internationally. A nice enough bunch of men, but no match for our side. Right, Mathias?"

He shrugged. "I don't know. We've never faced each other before. Aren't they backed by some newspaper or other?"

"Yes, not quite in our league, if you know what I mean."

Her interest sparked by the word "newspaper," Catherine squinted in order to make out faces of the opposing team a little more clearly. Of the four men, one was considerably taller than the others, and his face was definitely familiar. So . . . Michael Andrews also played polo. His presence would make it difficult for her to decide which team to root for. Was it proper, she wondered, to hope that both sides would win?

SHE WAS EXHAUSTED during the drive back to St. Cloud. It had been a fabulous experience to watch the polo game, and she could certainly see why Mathias enjoyed it so thoroughly. In some respects it was like ballet on horseback, but it was as ruthless as football as well.

Because The Wolves had won the game, Mathias was in very high humor all the way back to her home.

"You look a little pale, Catherine," he said finally. "Are you all right?"

"Yes," she replied. "But it was a bit much for me on the first day out, I guess. I suppose I'm not quite as well as I thought I was."

"Well, a good night's rest will fix you up, I'm sure. How do you happen to know that fellow on the other team?" The question came out casually, almost idly.

"We're neighbors."

"Really! Then it must've been hard on you to cheer for my side," he said nonchalantly.

"I took the lazy way out and didn't hope too hard for either team," she replied, laughing.

"That's easy enough to understand," Mathias said. "But if he's your neighbor, why haven't you ever been to a polo game before? Does he keep it a secret from everyone?"

"Michael? No, I don't think so. But we're really only getting to know each other," she explained, then told Mathias about their encounter earlier that week. "I hardly know him, as you can see."

"Hmm. It's hard to imagine a young reporter making enough money to live next door to your father."

Catherine glanced at Mathias's profile, noticing his high forehead and perfectly molded nose. "I really have no idea how much Michael earns. But the house belonged to his parents, and I suppose he inherited it when they died."

"You're probably right," he answered.

Something about his tone startled Catherine. It was as if Michael had been dismissed as being inconsequential.

Shortly thereafter, the roar of the car's powerful engine idled down to a purr as Mathias pulled into their driveway and parked in front of the house.

"Would you like to come in?" Catherine asked.

"No, thanks," he answered. "You're already tired, and I've got some work to do tonight. Your father's going to need some figures in the morning, and I'd better pull them together." His forearm left the wheel and leaned on the headrest behind Catherine. "I really should have had them ready on Friday, but . . . ." He broke off, letting his fingers play with her curly brown hair. "I haven't been able to get you out of my mind, Catherine. I knew five years ago that you would grow up to be a beauty, but I hadn't anticipated just how lovely and how warm you would be."

"Thank you," she said quietly, more than a little uncomfortable.

"May I kiss you?" he asked softly, his arm coming around her shoulder and pressing her toward him.

He didn't give her a chance to answer, however, and the next thing Catherine knew, he had enveloped her lips with his own. His kiss was pleasing, and she felt flattered that this debonair, older man would find her attractive. Mathias obviously could have had his choice of any woman in his social circle, all of them quite rich and strikingly attractive. That he should even notice her, particularly since she was so much younger and more unworldly than he, was quite appealing to her.

His lips pressed against hers lingeringly, and his left hand caressed her throat with a soft touch. She yielded readily until he began to pull her closer, his breath becoming ragged. Then she put her hands on his chest and pressed gently, pushing him away. "I'd better go in," she whispered when he let her go.

"Yes, I think you'd better, too. I'm not accustomed to sweet-smelling, clear-eyed young ladies, Catherine, and I don't want to lose control of myself."

She looked into his eyes to see if he was serious, but was unable to interpret their expression. "Thanks for a lovely afternoon," she said, opening the car door.

"Will I see you again?" His hand reached out to take hers for a moment.

"You'll be here tomorrow night," she replied, trying to laugh off his ardent gaze. "Aren't you working with father in the evening?"

He nodded, grimacing. "I'd forgotten. It's going to be torture, though, stuck in his stuffy den and knowing you're in the house somewhere."

"I could always go out," she said, unable to resist teasing him.

Mathias shook his head gravely. "I hope you don't. I want to see as much of you as I possibly can. Till tomorrow, then, sweet Catherine."

She watched his car turn around in the driveway, and waved when he pulled away. For some reason, she hated the thought of going back inside the house, but then she cheered herself with the knowledge that she'd be seeing him again the next evening. In many ways she found him to be a fascinating man—dashing, attractive and mature. The only men she'd ever dated before had been her own age, fellow students at the academy. It felt like a very different world when she was escorted by someone older and more sure of himself. Mathias seemed so totally at ease, so confident . . . and when he'd taken her in his arms, there had been no wish in her heart to stop him from kissing her.

Yes, Mathias Brunton was a new experience for her,

and she found him excitingly attractive. She started up the stairs to the front door. "Drat! I left the blanket and my coat in his car!" she said aloud.

Then she smiled. He'd be back tomorrow.

Chapter 5

The following morning was dreary. The sky was overcast with heavy, sagging clouds, and it had obviously rained during the night. As Catherine leaned out of her bedroom window, her eye was drawn toward the house next door. It was amazing how much Michael had accomplished in the past five days, she thought. Even though there were no flowers and the lawn had long ago become nothing but crabgrass, he had cleared out most of the weeds and undergrowth, and the yard had begun to show signs that someone cared for it.

As she noted the results of his labors, Michael himself came strolling out onto the terrace, sipping from a steaming cup. He was wearing a pair of brown whipcord trousers and a heavy crewneck sweater that seemed too tight around his arms and shoulders.

"Good morning," she called down, waving her hand to catch his eye.

He glanced around, then noticed the figure in the window next door. A warm, open smile crossed his face. "And good morning to you, Catherine," he replied. "Why are you still in your robe and pajamas?" he asked. "Half the morning is gone."

She shrugged helplessly. "Josephine insisted. When I went to bed last night, I was running about a millimeter of fever, and she decided I should sleep in today."

"Are you feeling any better? You looked rather tired yesterday afternoon."

Catherine nodded. "Much better, thanks. What about your leg?" She still remembered vividly how his horse had taken a nasty spill in the damp earth, momentarily pinning Michael beneath its ribs.

Michael laughed. "We sound like an old folks' home, comparing aches and pains." He flexed his leg so she could see that he was all right. "Good as new."

"I was terribly worried there for a moment," she remarked with a note of genuine concern in her voice.

"How long would it take you to get dressed?"

"Not long. Why?"

"I've got a cheese soufflé in the oven, and a spinach salad chilling. Instead of yelling at each other like this, why don't you come over and have brunch with me?"

"I'd love it," she replied. "Give me five minutes!"

"Your coffee will be waiting for you," he said, then waved and went back inside the house.

Catherine stepped swiftly out of her robe and enjoyed a quick shower. She was pulling on a pair of pantyhose when she remembered she'd have to get past Josephine, so she removed them and ran to her dresser to get a pair of knee-high woolen socks. She paused briefly in front of her closet to choose a pair of warm slacks, and she took down her heavy Irish sweater to wear over a rose and blue floral blouse.

Stepping back to look at herself in the mirror, she decided she'd be able to convince Josephine that she would be amply warm. Then, smiling, she ran into the

bathroom and combed out her curly brown hair, grateful that it never had to be put up in rollers even though
she often cursed it for being stubborn and willful.

Minutes later, she was rushing down the wide stairs
and heading for the kitchen.

"Where do you think you're going?" Josephine was
seated at the square kitchen table, a wary expression
in her eyes.

"Next door," Catherine answered. "I'm having
brunch with Michael."

"Before breakfast?" Mrs. Campbell had been standing at the sink, but she turned and gazed in astonish-
ment.

"That's what brunch is . . . a combination of breakfast and lunch," she explained, pirouetting in front of
her former governess. "I'm properly dressed, Josephine," she said, pulling up her pant leg to reveal her
warm socks. "And it's just next door."

Josephine shook her head. "Sometimes I think I was
happier when you were away at school. You probably
did the same crazy things, but at least I didn't have
to know about them!"

Catherine leaned down and hugged the older woman.
"I'll be back in an hour or so," she said.

"See that you keep that sweater on," Josephine called
after her as Catherine flew out the back door.

Seconds later, Catherine climbed over the low wall
that separated the two properties and went up onto
the terrace. She knew that Michael had seen her from
the kitchen window, so she didn't bother to knock at
the back door.

"That was fast," he said with a smile. "A woman
of your word, I see." He handed her a cup of coffee
turned a tan color with the hot milk he had added.

"Perfect," she said as she took it from him. "It smells divine, whatever you're cooking. I've never had brunch before, but I've read about them in American magazines."

He grinned, leading the way back into the spacious kitchen. "North Americans do a lot of things quite differently from the French," he said. "Have a seat. I hope you don't mind eating in here, but I didn't see the point setting a formal table."

"No, this is just fine, Michael." She glanced around and saw that the area had been decorated like a genuine country kitchen, complete with a raised hearth for indoor cooking. Café curtains bordered the large windows overlooking the backyard. "Where did you learn to cook?" she asked, watching him deftly open the oven door to check the soufflé.

"In the States," he replied, then gently closed the oven again. "My aunt and uncle had a small restaurant. First I learned how to peel onions and potatoes, and how to be a busboy, but little by little they taught me to cook and to manage the place."

"That must have been great fun for you," Catherine said, nodding appreciatively at the excellent coffee he'd made.

"Not really. I didn't like the work very much, and in the restaurant business you put in long, hard hours. But it's proved useful. I don't have to eat out or have the same thing every day."

"I'm impressed," she said sincerely. "I didn't think men even knew that houses came equipped with kitchens."

He twisted around and looked at her curiously. "Then why have the great chefs of the world always been men?"

"Of course, that was silly of me," she conceded. "So how did you become interested in being a reporter?"

Michael opened a drawer and took out knives and forks. "Watergate," he replied simply, setting the utensils on the round oak table. "I followed it like a soap opera, fascinated by how a couple of reporters could expose such a scandal. The impact of that—the drama and power, the responsibility of it all—well, I became hooked." He went over to a rough-hewn wooden hutch for plates and napkins. "I spoke to my aunt and uncle in 1972, explaining what it was I had to do, and they gave me their blessing. I got a job as a copyboy at the *Times*, and about a year later my city editor started sending me out on small assignments as a cub reporter."

"But weren't you awfully young for that kind of work?"

"Not really," Michael said, setting the table. "I had finished high school, after all, and was already taking night classes at City College. I would have gone to New York University, but I couldn't afford it on my salary."

"You must have been very good at it for them to have promoted you so fast," Catherine exclaimed with admiration.

Michael nodded, pleased. "I worked hard, I loved it, and I spent every waking moment living and breathing printers' ink and deadlines. I hung around the presses on my free time, and even volunteered as a printer's devil so I could know everything about the business. Later I started spending time at the French consulate in New York, hoping to pick up tidbits that might interest my city editor. Little by little, they gave me more responsibilities."

The buzz of a timer sounded and Michael rushed to the oven, opened the door cautiously, reached in and produced a golden soufflé. "It'll take a few minutes to cool before we can eat it," he said proudly.

"You really love your work, don't you?" Catherine said, sensing in him a kinship with how she felt about photography. She watched him as he sat down across from her, his angular face revealing a keen sensibility and his warm brown eyes radiating an inner strength and peace.

Michael looked at her evenly. "I love feeling that I'm a part of history, no matter how small. As life unfolds— politics, wars and weddings—I am a witness to it, and I help the rest of the world learn what's happening. It's a very rewarding way of life, Catherine."

"Then," she said as he pulled out a cigarette and lighted it, "you went on to *Paris Match*, right?"

"Just for a little while. I found I missed the pace of working on a daily paper. Besides, I'm not nearly as good at stringing words together as I am at getting to the core of a story. When you work for a magazine, you do interviews, of course, but most of the time you're tied to your desk writing up the story. I didn't care much for that. It just doesn't suit my temperament to be in one place all the time."

Catherine wrapped her small hands around her coffee cup, enjoying the warmth as it seeped through to her fingers. "I guess if I were a man, I'd probably feel the same way," she said.

Michael leaned back, laughing. "What has being a man got to do with it? Many women have led exciting lives, traveling all over the globe. Margaret Mead, Auriel

Durant, Margaret Bourke-White—to name only three. Your life is what you make of it, I think, and if you limit yourself before you've even begun—'' He raised his hands as if the rest of the sentence was self-explanatory.

Her dark blue eyes lingered on his lean, finely featured face. ''You really think it's that simple, Michael? Just . . . decide what you want to do, and then do it?''

He nodded slowly. ''Yes, I do. Maybe it's because I arrange my own life that way. But if you don't complicate your thinking with a lot of what ifs or maybes, I can't see that life is all that difficult. If you wanted to cross from this side of the road to the other, naturally you'd look both ways to be sure there's no oncoming traffic—but other than that, you just go ahead and cross the road. But if you start thinking about your posture or whether someone is watching you, you get tense and uncertain, and you probably decide to stay where you are.''

''You've given this a great deal of thought,'' she said softly.

''Yes, probably because I lost my parents when I was just a teenager. I had to face the reality of death, Catherine—the reality that, regardless of how secure you may think you are, it can all be taken away from you in shattering seconds. There isn't really any security in life, only an illusion of it. I guess that's why I became so mesmerized with the Watergate scandal, with the posturings of powerful people and the manipulations, both good and bad. It's also why I find my work so rewarding; it's real, it's happening now, and I'm a part of it.''

Catherine looked down at her cup, thinking over what he'd said. She didn't fully understand his point of view, for it seemed to her a very harsh, demanding way of looking at things. Suddenly, her project to take photographs for the annual report didn't seem all that interesting. Had her father been right? Were pictures just fluff, like icing on a cake, when what the shareholders really wanted were the facts? But then, not everyone could do the same things and hold the same opinions. *Perhaps,* she thought, *it's because I've never had to face life the way Michael has. Maybe I've still got a lot to learn.*

"Hungry?" Michael was leaning forward on his elbows, looking at her.

"Famished," she answered, smiling.

"Then brunch is coming up," he said, getting to his feet.

"How are you doing, getting the house back in shape?" she asked, watching him cut into the soufflé.

"It's coming," he said, putting the plates on the table then taking the salad out of the refrigerator and placing it between them. "I've got the dustcovers off almost all the furniture, but I've hired a cleaning team. They're coming in on Wednesday."

"They'll probably get it all done in a day," she said. "Mmm . . . this is superb!"

"Yes, it is good, isn't it?" he responded with a teasing glance. "Anyhow, even if I wanted to clean up the place by myself, I wouldn't be able to right away. The paper phoned this morning, asking if I'd interrupt my vacation for a special assignment."

"Something important?"

He gave a half laugh and nodded. "Not earthshaking, but more important than I usually get. They still treat me as if I'm too young to handle the bigger assignments, but this time they had no choice. Every one

of our senior reporters is out already, covering an equally
major assignment. They had no choice but to give me
a crack at the shah's visit."

"The Shah?" Her eyes grew wide.

"No, not *the* shah," he replied, amused. "This one
is the head of an emerging country that no one's ever
heard of. But you've obviously not been following the
news lately."

"I'm afraid not," she admitted guiltily, knowing that
she would have to pay closer attention to it since she
was starting to value her new friendship with Michael.
"It certainly is confusing."

"Well, if you haven't been keeping up, it's like walking into a theater during the performance. You don't
know who any of the characters are, or what they're
talking about. The news happens every day, Catherine—it's not going to wait for you to have some spare
time."

She bristled slightly. "It isn't as important to everyone as it is to you, Michael."

He looked at her from beneath his brows, then smiled
slowly. "I wasn't being critical of you, Catherine, I was
just making an observation."

Softening, she realized that her reaction had been
a defensive one. She didn't like feeling uninformed in
his company, and instead of accepting the blame for
it herself, she had turned her anger on him. "I'm sorry,"
she said quietly. "I guess I have some catching up to
do."

"I'm sorry, too," Michael said. "Sometimes I forget
that not everyone shares my belief that what's going
on in the world is so vitally important. Lots of people
live in total indifference and seem to be just as happy
for it."

Anxious to show him that her flare-up hadn't been serious, Catherine said, "Yes, and when a war breaks out and their sons are sent to fight, they don't have any idea of why the young men are risking their lives."

He nodded. "More often than not, neither do the soldiers themselves. It's tragic, really. If I had to die for my country, I'd want to know why, wouldn't you?"

"Of course," she said emphatically.

"We're getting awfully serious, I'm afraid. I hadn't meant for that to happen," he said cheerfully. "Ready for some salad?" He dished some crisp spinach leaves onto a small plate, digging around in the bowl to be sure she had enough pieces of bacon and chopped egg. After serving himself, he said smugly, "This is one of my specialties."

"You're going to make some woman an awfully good husband," Catherine said, laughing.

"No apron strings for me," he joked. "But then, no reporters should ever get married anyhow—they should be footloose, and free to travel at a moment's notice. But what about you? What are you planning to do with your life now that school's over?"

Briefly Catherine told him about her studies and her hopes of becoming a commercial photographer. "I just haven't quite decided what kind of photography interests me most," she added, leaning back in her chair as she watched him polish off the last of his salad.

"I'd suggest the newspaper field, except that there's really no money in it. It's a labor of love and little more."

"Well, happily, I don't have to rush into any decision. I've been thinking I might live at home for a few months, try out different types of work, and see if anything holds my interest."

"Doesn't it bother you to be living at home with your father? I should think you'd want to get out on your own, without having to check back with dad."

"Oh, I've been able to do that pretty well while I was at school. Besides, he really doesn't pay all that much attention to my comings and goings. 'I've raised you, Catherine,' " she said with a falsely deep voice, hunching up her shoulders and tucking in her chin, " 'to be a proper young lady. I don't expect to have to be your warden now that you're grown-up.' "

Michael laughed. "Well, that's pretty liberal for the old fellow."

"You say that as if you don't like him," she said, somewhat surprised. It had never occurred to her that other people besides herself might see his austere attitudes as less than desirable.

"I don't really know your dad," Michael said. "As a boy, I found him nice enough but very distant. When my folks were killed, he did send a note of condolence—but it was rather stiff. Years ago, I'd sometimes think about you and wonder how you stood living with him. My own parents were warm and loving, and I never saw your dad showing you any warmth or affection. I don't mean to offend you, Catherine, and I hope I've not spoken out of turn—"

"No, no! I'm just taken aback, I guess. Josephine never says anything about him that might lessen him in my eyes, and the only other feedback I've ever had was from his cousin Roberta. But she's very fond of father, so I can't accept her opinions of him as objective."

Michael lighted a cigarette, stretching his arm behind him to get an ashtray from the hutch. "You must have spent a lot of years feeling guilty for not liking him," he said softly.

Catherine gazed into his eyes, his words reverberating in her mind. "Not liking him? But I . . . ." She stopped short, unable to say the words she knew she should. "I'd never thought of it before," she said instead, "but maybe you're right. I love my father, Michael, but love and like aren't quite the same, are they?"

"No," he answered simply. "One often has little to do with the other."

"I guess I've never got close enough to find out if I like him or not."

He blew a puff of smoke upward over her head, then looked at her compassionately. "But the child in you must have resented that, don't you think? And then the resentment built up. . . . It's pretty hard to like someone you resent."

"You're very perceptive, Michael," she said slowly, appreciating the gentle way he had led her to see something she had never contemplated before. The way he had broached the subject made it seem all right, as if she were perfectly normal to view her father differently from how most other children viewed theirs. He was, after all, quite different from most other fathers she'd met. Michael's gentleness left her feeling that it was not she who was abnormal, but her father; and that comforted her considerably.

He casually glanced at the kitchen clock. Catherine, now totally attuned to this new friend, observed his gesture and realized it was time for her to leave.

"But don't you want some more coffee?" Michael stood up after she did, a surprised look in his brown eyes.

"No, I've already taken up too much of your time. You have work to do, and I'm just the next-door convalescent. Thanks for the wonderful lunch, Michael . . . and for the first stimulating conversation I've had in months." She extended her hand.

Michael accepted it, but covered her hand with both of his own. "It was fun for me, too, Catherine. If I can wind up my assignment, how about catching a movie with me this Sunday? Mind you, though," he added, laughing apologetically, "I might have to break the date at the last minute."

She was tempted to say she'd love to, but she suddenly remembered that she'd promised to watch Mathias play polo again on Sunday afternoon. "I can't," she said. "Maybe one day during the week?"

"Great. Would you mind if it was a last-minute invitation? I never know for sure where I'll be. Otherwise I wouldn't dream of being so vague."

"I don't mind, Michael. After all, we're friends, aren't we?"

"Yes, and I think we're going to be good friends, too."

He showed her to the door, and the brisk air tingled on her skin as she walked back to her own home. Before going inside, she turned and saw that Michael was still standing on the terrace, waiting to make sure that she made it indoors. She smiled and waved at him.

As she climbed the stairs to her own room, she met Josephine, who was coming down. "Did you have a nice time?"

"Exceptionally," Catherine replied, feeling strangely secure and alive.

Chapter 6

The following Monday Catherine was up bright and early having breakfast with her father so she could drive to Moreau Electronics with him. Her camera bag, already packed and waiting on the bench near the front door, was crammed with rolls of color and black-and-white film as well as her flash, tripods and two sets of mounted movie lights. She was prepared for any situation inside the plant; though bounced lighting could be very effective for some shots, she knew that machinery had a tendency to reflect light and would require the more manageable mounted lights. Her bag looked more like what a backpacker ready to traverse the frozen Alaskan tundra would have, than what a photographer would ordinarily carry.

"I understand you went out with Mathias again yesterday," Mr. Moreau said, extricating a wedge of grapefruit with his spoon.

"Yes," she replied, pulling off the tip of a hot croissant and buttering it. "I'm really finding polo an exciting sport, and Mathias is virtually a star in the set. He's a seven-goal man, did you know that?"

"I suppose that's good," her father replied tersely.

"Do you think it is wise to be seeing him so often? He's been coming here almost every evening for supper, and he might think your interest rather unseemly."

She tried to smile. "I didn't press my company on him, father, he invited me. Besides, once supper's finished, the two of you locked yourselves up in your den. It isn't as if we're socializing. . . ."

"Perhaps not," he replied grudingly, "but I don't wish to find myself in the middle of any awkward situations. Mathias is very important to the firm, and I don't want you interfering in any way. Is that clear, Catherine?"

"Who are you trying to protect, father? Him or me?"

"Myself, if you must know. Are you finding yourself attracted to him, Catherine? In a serious way, that is?"

She tried to keep her voice light. "Well, he's very attractive, don't you agree? But I do think it's a bit soon to be discussing anything more than our having a good time."

"He's ten years your senior, Catherine."

"So were you to mother." The words were out before she knew it, and she could have kicked herself for saying them.

Mr. Moreau's head came up abruptly and his gray eyes turned to steel as he looked at his daughter. His mouth formed a straight line beneath his graying mustache as he said, "I am not the topic of this discussion, Catherine, you are. Frankly, I would be most pleased if you and Mathias were to consider marriage. If I had to select a husband for you, I would be a fool not to think of Mathias Brunton as the right man. He has a good career ahead of him and I have never had any reason to question his integrity."

"You're not suggesting . . .?"

"I suggest nothing, Catherine. You've already dem-
onstrated your capacity to do as you please and ignore
my wishes. I am merely stating a fact. Mathias would
make a good husband for you, and I would like to
know you are in good hands. Besides, I might even
trust him enough in time to let him assume the business. At least he's not an irresponsible vagabond," Mr.
Moreau said flatly.

Catherine was instantly on the alert. Had Josephine
mentioned to her father that Michael had called for
her on Wednesday and had taken her to a movie? No,
that wasn't likely. Josephine had never squealed on
her before, and she didn't think she would now. Catherine knew full well, however, that her father would
think poorly of her dating a mere reporter, no matter
how good his background was.

Her mind drifted back to that evening with Michael
and what a good time she had had. The movie had
been an old Ingmar Bergman film, crammed with sym-
bolism; and while she had enjoyed the cinematic ef-
fects, the story had left her somewhat bewildered.
Later they had gone to a small coffeehouse, and over
cappuccino laced with brandy, she'd been vastly re-
lieved to learn that it hadn't made any sense to Michael,
either.

They had laughed a good deal that evening, and
she'd cajoled him into telling her more about America.
When it grew late, Michael had tucked her into his
five-year-old sedan and had driven her home. Ignoring
the fact that he lived right next door, Michael had
pulled the noisy car up to her front door and had
walked with her up the steps. He had shaken her hand
briefly, had said they would have to try a comedy next

time, and then got back into his car and gone home. The courtesy was a small gesture, but Catherine had appreciated the fact that he had treated her with respect and not just like the kid next door.

It occurred to her that she was being secretive about seeing him, and she wondered why she should feel that way. Michael was certainly a very presentable young man, so why was she trying to keep her father from finding out that they had dated? Catherine didn't know, but it bothered her.

"Well, are you ready?" Mr. Moreau rose from the table and pulled his vest down snugly around his waist.

She glanced down at her place and realized she had eaten her breakfast automatically without tasting anything. "Yes, whenever you are."

"Then let's be on our way. Factories work on time schedules, Catherine, and I don't like to be late. It sets a bad example for my employees."

MOREAU ELECTRONICS WAS a sprawling, one-story edifice, taking up a little more than an acre. Catherine had only been to the place once before, shortly after it was built. It had been a big decision for her father— whether he should expand his original factory or take the plunge and build an entirely new and modern plant. It had been one of the first buildings to utilize solar heating, and it had been considered quite daring at the time it was built.

Despite its pale yellow concrete facade, the factory had a pleasant air about it, lent by the old trees that had been left standing around it and the fact that the Forest d'Armainvilliers was nearby. So many corporations chopped down everything in sight to make room for parking lots, Catherine thought, with the end result that their buildings looked more like prisons than places where people could enjoy their work. But her father had decided to work the parking area around the trees. Well-tended lawns surrounded the structure, and there were picnic tables, which the employees used during the summer months. The facility had been a thoughtful gesture on Mr. Moreau's part, and Catherine remembered being surprised—even at sixteen she had realized that he wasn't given to thinking of others.

When they entered the lobby, a security guard held the door for them. Catherine smiled at the man, but he remained stoically at attention. They passed the receptionist, and again her father made no effort to introduce her. For a moment Catherine wondered if it was because she was carrying all her equipment and that he might be embarrassed by it. But as they walked through the maze of offices in the front of the building, she caught glimpses of various executives and realized that they were all busily at work, hunched over their desks or talking on telephones.

Mr. Moreau paused in front of some swinging double doors and told her to wait for him. She watched as he entered the shipping room area and walked over to a punch clock. He removed a time card, inserted it in the clock, then put it back in the slot. When he rejoined her, Catherine's eyes were wide with disbelief. "Surely you don't punch in, father!"

He glanced at her only briefly. "I certainly do. I expect everyone else to do it, and it's only fair that I conform to the rules."

She smiled, shaking her head as she lifted her camera bag and caught up with him. "And are you docked if you're late?"

"As a matter of fact, yes," he replied. "For tax purposes, I am on the payroll here, the same as any other employee. Regardless of what you may sometimes think, Catherine, I'm a fair and just man. I work hard, and I expect others to do likewise. When I make a company policy, I also obey it. I do not believe in executive privileges—they're counterproductive to the total work effort."

Soon they made a turn to the left and went down a short corridor to her father's office. It was no larger than any of the others, but it did feel different. In some of the offices they had passed, Catherine had seen photographs of smiling wives and children, or pictures of pets; several offices had potted plants cheering them up; and others had colorful posters breaking up the drab feeling given by the beige office furniture and walls. There was other evidence of individuals impressing their own personalities on their surroundings, but not in her father's office. Other than the view of the forest from his window, his room was efficiently stark. Even the filing cabinets were in the adjoining room where his secretary sat.

Mr. Moreau crossed over to his desk and flipped through the telephone messages, then rang for his secretary. The woman was about forty, neatly dressed in a manner to avoid distraction, and she entered the room briskly, saying, "Good morning, Mr. Moreau."

"Mrs. Simpson, this is my daughter, Catherine," he replied brusquely, ignoring her salutation.

The woman turned and smiled pleasantly as Mr. Moreau went on. "She's going to be taking photographs of the factory, so it might be wise for someone to give her an orientation tour. She already knows Mathias Brunton, but she should meet the foreman for

each division. You'll also want to arrange a security
I.D. pass for her so she can come and go as she wishes."

"Yes, sir," the woman replied, leaving the room.

"As for you, Catherine, you're on your own now.
I have a great deal to get done this morning and won't
have time to show you around myself. Moreover, I'm
having lunch with Roberta today, so I may be a little
late getting back this afternoon."

"You're going to drive all the way to Paris for lunch?"

"She's been lonely, as you know, since my brother
died. I try to have lunch with her at least once a week,
and I take her out to dinner a few times a month."

"I should think you'd have better things to do with
your time," Catherine muttered to herself.

"What's that?"

"I said, I'm sure you two have a very good time,"
Catherine fibbed. She'd never liked Roberta, though
she could never figure out precisely why that was so.
There was something false about the woman, she felt,
something apart from her face-lift and the styles she
wore to make herself look younger. Perhaps it was her
tight, almost piercing voice, or her way of laughing
even when something wasn't genuinely funny. Roberta was one of those people who used endearments
without discrimination and she was given to the edi-
torial "we." She never said that Catherine looked lovely
in a dress—she always said, "Don't we look lovely
today." It was a little thing, but one of the many little
things that had always grated on Catherine's nerves.

"Did you hear me, Catherine?"

Her father's voice brought her abruptly to the present. "I'm sorry, father . . . I guess my mind was wan-
dering."

He exhaled heavily, tucking in the corners of his

mouth with displeasure. "I was conveying Roberta's regards to you, and the fact that she'd like you to have lunch with her some day next week. She wondered if you might like to spend the afternoon shopping in Paris."

Catherine had to laugh. "I never 'go shopping,' father. If I need a sweater, I buy one. The thought of trekking from store to store, trying things on in front of hovering salesclerks, is my idea of torture."

"Then you had better overcome your attitude. I mentioned to her that you had been seeing quite a bit of Mathias, going to polo games and all that, and she said that you would need some new clothes if you were going to be in such stylish company."

"Father, I'm not seeing quite a bit of Mathias . . . *you* are. I've only gone out with him twice. The fact that he's been to the house every evening for the past week and that I happened to be there is coincidental. I really don't need any new clothes right now, and even if I did, Roberta's idea of chic is a far cry from my own."

"Be that as it may," Mr. Moreau said soberly, "I expect you to extend every courtesy to Roberta. Since she has been kind enough to take an interest in you, to go with you to some of the better stores and offer her advice, I'd appreciate it if you would cooperate. She's quite fond of you, Catherine, and always has been."

"It's my duty, I suppose, to have lunch with her, father. But you'd be throwing your money away on some of those fancy boutiques in Paris. What if I never go to another match? I'll have a lot of fancy clothes and nowhere to wear them."

Mr. Moreau sat down at his desk, rubbing his temples. "You can be the most exasperating child," he said quietly. "Most girls your age would be thrilled to have their fathers offer to buy them new wardrobes. But not you."

"I don't wish to seem ungrateful, please understand that. But Roberta is only interested in designer clothes. The label means more to her than whether or not the outfit looks good. If you're willing to spend that kind of money, I'd far prefer to have a Hasselblad camera."

Her father frowned. "You won't catch a suitable husband with a camera! A man wants to know that his wife can dress well, and always appropriately for the occasion!"

So that was it, Catherine realized. Roberta had been filling his head with stories about the wealthy polo set. Obviously the two of them had been discussing her relationship with Mathias. She knew there was no way out of it then; she'd have to go along with it if only to keep peace. "All right, father," she said, trying to sound cheerful at the prospect. "Please tell Roberta that I appreciate her interest, and I'll call her one day next week."

"That's better," he said gruffly. "I shall never understand why you have to be coerced into everything, Catherine."

She was tempted to say that it was only because he was always trying to run her life and make her do things she didn't want to do, but she managed to remain silent. Fortunately, Mrs. Simpson came in at that moment with Mathias right behind her.

"Here's your security pass, Miss Moreau," the woman said, then turned to her employer. "Mr. Barrie in London is trying to reach you, sir. Shall I put the call through?"

"What does he want now," Mr. Moreau said tightly. "Never mind, put him through." He waved his hand, dismissing his secretary and gesturing to Mathias to take his daughter away with him.

Catherine hefted her camera case, which Mathias immediately took from her, and they left the room. "My office is down here," he said, pulling the door closed behind him. "Have you had any coffee yet?"

It was such a relief to get away from her father that Catherine would have readily agreed to a cup of hemlock. "Earlier," she said, "but I'd adore some now."

"I'll have my secretary get you some," he said, pushing open the door to his office. Beyond it, a small open area of desks could be seen, all of them occupied by secretaries. "Oh, Katie, would you get some coffee for my guest?"

"I'm working on a report for Mr. Atkins, sir."

"C'mon, you can take a few minutes out—just for me, Katie?" His baritone was cajoling and boyishly charming.

The woman nodded and got up from her desk. Catherine watched her absently, wondering why Mathias had said she was his secretary when it was so obvious that she belonged to a secretarial pool.

The telephone on his desk rang, and Mathias suggested she take a seat while he answered it.

Instead, Catherine looked around the room, examining the framed photo of Mathias on Windfire, his mallet resting on his shoulder. Another showed Mathias lined up with the members of The Wolves, and others were taken during the game itself. In one picture, she noted that Lady Georgina Dickinson was handing him a trophy, a knowing smile on her long, thin face. Interspersed among the pictures were sundry ribbons Mathias had won for his horsemanship.

In the meantime she couldn't help overhearing Mathias's end of the telephone conversation.

"No, Frank, the old man will never go for it. What? No, really, I know what I'm talking about. What you're suggesting is tantamount to a kickback, and Moreau would drop dead if I even hinted at such a thing. Sure, I know it's different these days, but he doesn't know that. Well, maybe you and I can work out something between us. If you're going to lay a five-hundred-thousand-dollar order on us, I'm sure there must be some way we can arrange for you and your wife to get down to Cannes for a few days. Okay, Frank. Let it ride for a day or two, and I'll see what I can come up with. Sure, Frank, anytime."

He put the receiver back as Katie came in with a plastic tray holding two cups of coffee, sugar and milk. She put it down on the corner of the desk and left wordlessly.

"I'm sorry for the interruption," Mathias said with a big smile. "Some of our customers really expect a lot for their money, but that's the job of an account executive. Got to keep the customers happy, right?"

"I suppose so," Catherine answered, pouring some milk into her cup and stirring. "I gather that he wants a free vacation at father's expense. Is that really how things are done?"

Mathias shrugged. "Money is tight these days, and our clients know it. If we want their business, well, you have to extend yourself in a competitive world. He rubs our back, we rub his. Simple."

"But father wouldn't approve?"

"No. He's pretty old-fashioned in some ways, so I have to work around him quite a bit. If he knew how often I've saved this company's neck by bending the rules—well, he wouldn't like it. You won't tell on me, will you?"

She felt curiously torn about his question, but realized she knew nothing of the corporate world. "As long as it's only bending them, I guess not," she said. "Besides, it's apparently good for business."

"Of course it is, Catherine," Mathias said, taking her free hand and squeezing it. "This will be just our little secret, okay? Moreau Electronics means a great deal to me, and I'd never do anything to hurt it. For that matter, it's one of the reasons I play polo—you'd be amazed at how many clients I've picked up at the matches. The right people, Catherine, can put you onto a lot of very good leads."

"I'm glad I'm a photographer," Catherine replied, laughing. "I'd make a terrible account executive."

"No, you wouldn't, not with those beautiful eyes of yours." He moved closer to her then, until their faces were almost touching. "You're a very special person, Catherine, and I turn into putty whenever you're around."

She pulled out of his arms as gently as she could, surprised that Mathias would be so ardent in full view of the secretaries beyond. "I'm supposed to be introduced to the foremen," she said, changing the subject.

"Right, and I'm going to be your escort. Then, for lunch, there's a wonderful little inn not too far from here. Since your father also has a lunch date, you and

I can have a leisurely time and not worry about getting back on the dot.''

"But aren't you going to be docked?"

Mathias winked at her conspiratorially. "I have a friend in accounting. She's only twenty, but she keeps hoping I'll ask her out on a date."

Catherine realized she had two secrets to keep from her father. He'd be livid if he knew that Mathias didn't get docked the same as everyone else did.

Mathias crossed the room and closed the door with his foot, then picked up his coffee and sat down behind his desk. "Do you really have to carry all that stuff around all the time?"

She followed his glance to her camera bag, with the tripods strapped to its bottom and the movie-light bars resting between the grips. "No," she answered, smiling. "I just didn't know what I'd be running into with this job, so I came fully prepared. If there's a safe in the building, I'll leave the bulk of it here each evening."

"There's a safe in your father's office," he said, blowing on his coffee, "but it's too small to hold all of that. Tell you what, I'll keep it here inside my office and lock up every night. I usually lock it anyhow, so it won't be any inconvenience."

"If you're sure you won't mind," she said.

"Mind? Not at all, Catherine. I like the idea of your being dependent upon me."

She smiled, and for some inane reason, her mind drifted to Michael Andrews. If there was anything Michael did *not* want, it was someone dependent upon him. She glanced at Mathias's sandy blond hair, his perfect features and his impeccable suit. He looked every inch like an executive on his way up . . . whereas when she had first seen Michael she had thought he was a gardener. Perhaps her father was correct after all . . . clothes obviously did make an enormous difference in the impression one made.

"Well? Shall we begin your tour?"

"By all means," she answered, wondering why she hadn't heard from Michael in the past few days. . . .

Chapter 7

April gave way to May, and by the fifteenth, the trees were a hazy green and people were already out of doors planting flowers or beginning their vegetable gardens. The earth smelled clean, the scent of spring flowers filled the air in St. Cloud, and everyone seemed to have happy smiles and cordial greetings for one another. The dreariness of winter was past, and no one mourned it.

Catherine was once again back to her usual good health, and even Josephine no longer admonished her to keep warm or avoid overexertion.

Her work at the factory was finished, and just that morning she had completed the layout for the annual report. The publication, she knew, was going to be very handsome, and she was justifiably proud of herself. She'd used halftones in elongated vertical positions throughout the text, but vivid color photographs broke up the sections of the report. Several photos were close-ups of the workers wearing magnifying glasses as they welded the intricate and equally colorful circuitry to thin aluminum bases; in others, by slowing down the shutter speed, she had captured the move-

ment of the conveyor belts carrying boxes upon boxes
of completed products inexorably toward their desti-
nations.

Every phase of the factory's work, except the most
boring or visually uninteresting, had been captured by
Catherine's camera. On a particularly warm day, she'd
taken candid photos of employees having lunch at the
tables out of doors, with some of the men playing
handball in the background. The report, which was
sent to all the shareholders, would give everyone a
clear concept of what Moreau Electronics manufac-
tured and what kind of people worked there.

Mr. Moreau had kept himself very removed from
what she was doing, and seemed interested only in
seeing to it that her presence at the plant didn't disrupt
the work flow. But Mathias had shown considerable
interest in her work, and on several occasions had
stayed late with her to decide which photos to use in
the report.

She'd come to rely upon Mathias's opinions about
the layout, and she frequently questioned him about
where she could break up the typeset material so that
readers wouldn't be confused. She knew that the purpose of the report was to provide information, and she
wanted the report to read clearly. Happily, he proved
to be very adept at grasping what she wanted to convey
and had made some very cogent suggestions.

Catherine had also been seeing quite a bit of Mathias
socially. He had introduced her to members of his club,
and—outfitted with her new designer clothes—she had
been readily accepted by the men. Her success with
the women, with rare exception, had been more sub-
dued. Apparently Mathias was the best dancer avail-
able to any type of music, and the women vied for his

talents. With Catherine around, he wasn't quite as free to extend his invitations. Fortunately, though, Georgie Dickinson had decided to pull in her claws, and while Catherine still didn't like the woman, she no longer had to defend herself.

It's strange, she thought, putting the completed layout inside her briefcase, *how much my life has changed in just six weeks*. There were times when she felt as if she'd always known Mathias Brunton. He was a wonderful escort, amusing, charming and very attentive. They went to only the best restaurants and the most chic clubs; Catherine was even becoming accustomed to seeing herself in the society pages of the Paris newspapers. Initially she'd been shocked by this, and from time to time had even felt that her privacy was being intruded upon. But Mathias convinced her otherwise, eventually making her feel that it was her responsibility to be photographed. "Think of the poor people who live vicariously," he had said one evening.

Her thoughts were suddenly interrupted by a knock on the door and a masculine voice calling, "Hello? Anybody home?"

Startled, Catherine glanced over her shoulder toward the kitchen door. "Michael! Where have you been all these weeks?" She stood up, went to the door, and unlatched it for him.

He grinned, stepping inside and looking around. "Looks like you're working, Catherine. I can come back, if you like."

"Oh, no, you don't," she replied, laughing. "I've been wondering what you've been up to, and you're not leaving here until I get an explanation." She scooped up the scraps of paper and trimmed photos from the table and put them in the garbage container under the sink. "I've been working in here because there's more space than in my room, but I'm finished now. Want some coffee?"

"Sure, why not?" He leaned against the refrigerator, his arms folded as he watched her fill the kettle and plug it in "Is that the job for your dad?"

Catherine nodded. "All done now. . . . I'm taking it over to the printer in a little while. Want to come along?"

"I shouldn't," he said, his brown eyes twinkling, "but I will. How have you been? You're looking great, Catherine. Sometimes you're a dead ringer for your mother, do you know that?"

"Do you remember her?" Catherine turned and stared at him.

"Pretty well," he replied. "I remember that she was beautiful and that she had a smile that made a rainy day seem sunny."

"I hardly remember her at all," Catherine said, a slight frown on her forehead. "But I was only eleven when she died."

"Well, so what have you been up to lately?" Michael asked, obviously wishing to change the subject.

"Oh, work mostly. But you still haven't told me where you've been."

He shrugged. "I was in Beirut for a couple of weeks, then *L'Express* sent me to West Berlin on a story. I just go back last night," he explained. "Didn't you get my postcards?"

"No," she answered, surprised. "How many did you send?"

"Only two, one from each place. I didn't want you to think I'd fallen off the face of earth. But that's the mail for you! They'll probably arrive in another six weeks or so."

She smiled as she got out two cups and placed them on the sideboard. "I've missed you, Michael. Though we haven't known each other very long, I've come to expect seeing you."

He moved over to the table, pulled out a chair and sat down. "There's something different about you, Catherine—you seem somehow, well, more sophisticated, surer of yourself."

Catherine scooped out spoonfuls of instant coffee and poured boiling water from the kettle into the cups. "Maybe I am," she answered casually. "I've been doing a lot of socializing since I last saw you."

"Is that a new outfit you're wearing?"

"No, but father did insist that I buy a lot of new clothes. I'm feeling quite the debutante these days."

Michael laughed. "You? You'd never hang around with that crowd of phonies!"

"I'm not hanging around, as you say, with phonies, Michael. They're all very nice people, urbane and clever."

He gazed at her seriously for a few seconds, then accepted the cup she handed to him. "I'm sure they are," he said after a moment. "By the way, are you free this evening? Would you like to go to a small bistro for supper, and maybe take the subway over to the Left Bank and browse through the bookstalls?"

"What happened to your car?" she asked, a little taken aback at the thought of getting on the subway. But then she checked herself, realizing she'd been spoiled by Mathias and his sleek sports car.

"It's in the shop. I tried to start her up this morning

and all I got was a groan. You don't mind taking the subway, do you?"

"No, no, not at all," she answered, ashamed of herself for a moment. She actually did mind, and it was the last thing in the world she would ever have expected of herself. Hadn't she taken trains and buses all during her school years? However, she admitted, she no longer wore any of her older clothes unless she was up to her elbows in work. *It's true*, she said to herself silently, *in just these past few weeks, I have changed*. A bistro instead of an elegant restaurant? Browsing around the Left Bank instead of going to a lavish party or a gallery opening? Could six weeks have made such a difference? Apparently it had.

"You look as if you can't quite make up your mind," he said, tilting his head toward her questioningly. "Do you want to go out tonight or not?"

"Of course, Michael," she said, laughing. "I guess seeing you so unexpectedly has caught me off balance. I'd love it. . . . I haven't been over in that part of town for ages."

He beamed. "Good. I have a chum who lives just off the Boulevard St. Germain. He and his wife are struggling along while he's finishing his first novel, but I think you'd like them. They're very sincere and open people, and I know they'll like you."

"Wonderful," she said, but she was already wondering if they really would like her. She had learned around Mathias to be more diplomatic than before, saying the right thing instead of what was on her mind. After all, it was important for her to make a good impression. As Mathias had pointed out, it was through those connections that he managed to get new business for Moreau Electronics.

They chatted on while they finished their coffee, and Michael told her about some of the work he'd been doing while he was out of the country. "They're beginning to trust me more," he said, tilting back in his chair. "I'm getting better and meatier assignments, and I know the city editor is considering me for a couple of feature stories."

"That's marvelous, Michael," she said enthusiastically. "But the idea of your being in Beirut right now, especially after what happened to your parents . . . well, it's scary."

He nodded seriously. "Yeah, it sort of spooked me, too, when I first arrived. But I got over it. It's like getting back on the horse that's thrown you—just something you have to do if you don't want to be a quitter."

"Speaking of which," she said, keenly aware of his easy manner and candid expression, "have you been playing much polo lately?"

"No. When would I? But polo's just something I do for fun, anyway. It's not as if The Bennetts would ever be serious competition for anyone. It's a good way to get some exercise and fresh air, but none of us on the paper is as dedicated to the sport as some other teams are—we can't devote enough time to it."

"I'm becoming quite an expert on the game," she said, smiling.

"With that same fellow I saw you with when we played The Wolves?"

Catherine nodded. "Yes, he plays every chance he gets and I tag along." Almost immediately she felt guilty. Why had she phrased it that way? Why hadn't she just said that she was seeing Mathias, and leave it at that? "Anyhow, shall we get going? I promised

to deliver the layout to Mr. Schultz by noon, and I've
got to get Mrs. Campbell's car back to her early enough
for her to do the marketing."

"Sure, let's go."

They left the house. Even though Michael pushed
the passenger seat back as far as it would go, his legs
were still cramped in the small car, but he took the
situation with a sense of humor. During the drive, he
drew Catherine out on her activities, and she cheerfully
told him how she was now part of a social set, going
places and doing things she'd never expected would
ever be a part of her life.

"But you seem to be enjoying it," he said while they
waited for a traffic light to turn green. "You're posi-
tively bubbling."

"Well, it *is* very exciting, Michael." She put the car
into first gear and pulled out with the rest of the traffic.
"I've led such a cloistered existence most of my
life . . . of course I'm having a lot of fun. Wouldn't
you?"

"Maybe," he responded hesitantly. "I've been to a
few gatherings like that, but I didn't like them very
much. But if you'd been with me, I might have felt
differently."

"I feel as if I'm in a fairy tale," Catherine exclaimed
enthusiastically. "Meeting Lord So-and-so or the
Duchess of Such-and-such . . . . Mathias and I have
even been invited to a fox hunt next month."

"Really," Michael said dryly. "Nice for you, but not
so happy for the fox. Have you any idea what a fox
hunt is really like, Catherine?"

She glanced at him from the corner of her eye. "I've
never been to one before."

He nodded. "They're barbarous. Hunters and hounds

alike stampeding the small creature, terrifying it—the fox knows it's running for its life, Catherine. It's not at all uncommon for the poor animal's heart to burst out of sheer terror."

"You're exaggerating," Catherine said, shocked.

Michael shook his head. "You'll find out for yourself, I guess." He pulled out a cigarette and lit it, then rolled the window down a little. "How's your father, by the way?"

She was still a little shaken by what Michael had said, but she tried to put it out of her mind. "Oh, he's fine, I suppose. I've been so busy lately that we hardly see each other. But he's still the same taciturn, withdrawn man I've always known."

"I've been wondering," Michael said, taking a slow drag from his cigarette, "if after your mother's death, your father changed a great deal. The woman I remember would never have married someone with his present personality."

"I've thought about that, too, sometimes," Catherine said, feeling strangely sad for a moment. "I wish she were alive, Michael. There's so much I'd like to know about." They drove along the Rue de Bercy past the Lyon railway station as she added, "I get a little confused sometimes, as if too much is happening too fast. If she were still alive, I'd be able to consult with her. . . . There's Josephine, of course, and I love her dearly, but she's much too old for me to fully confide in. And of late, it's as if there's a gap growing between us, as if she's annoyed with me. But if my mother were around . . . ."

"What did she die of?" Michael asked quietly.

Catherine maneuvered the small car around the station, then edged her way onto the Avenue Ledru-

Rollin. "It's been a long time since my father told me . . . pneumonia, I think."

"Won't he talk about her?"

"Never! He turns into an iceberg at the slightest mention of her!"

"Where is she buried then?"

"I don't know," Catherine said with a short little laugh. "Isn't that funny? I have no idea what cemetery she's in! I'd never thought about that before. If I did know, I could at least go to her graveside and commune with her in my heart."

"Wouldn't Josephine tell you?"

"I doubt it. I think my father has given her orders never to discuss my mother with me. Whenever I'd ask her about my mother, even when I was a teenager, Josephine would either change the subject or get very busy elsewhere. No, I don't think she'd tell me."

"Well, then, what if I find out for you?"

Catherine swallowed hard, pulled over to the curb, then looked at Michael intently. "Would you? Could you? I'd be so grateful, Michael!"

He grinned and patted her hand as it rested on the steering wheel. "I happen to hate mysteries, Catherine. There's bound to be a record in the newspaper morgue. Vital statistics, that sort of thing."

"Even though we live in St. Cloud?"

"Why not? Your father is a prominent man, after all. I can at least check it out for you. Okay?"

"Oh, Michael," she said, throwing her arms around his neck, "I'd be so happy! Anything, anything at all that you can find out . . . it would make me feel a little closer to her!"

"Hey! Take it easy! Do you want me to get a swelled

head?" He gave her a brief hug, then disentangled her arms, laughing at her ebullience.

Her eyes were misted as she looked at him. "You're the only person I know who seems to understand how I feel, Michael. Thank you for your friendship. . . ."

Michael's warm brown eyes were tender as he gazed at her. "Maybe it's because I've been lonely, too, Catherine," he said softly.

Impulsively, she leaned over and kissed his cheek. Even though she knew that Josephine loved her deeply, it wasn't the same as having Michael's quiet compassion and caring. He seemed to know what she was feeling without even being told, and as she steered the car back into the traffic, her heart was filled with gratitude toward him. Even an impersonal grave was more than she'd had to remember her mother by in the past. Somehow, some way, Catherine was certain that Michael would help her, even though he had plenty to do in his own life. A bittersweet smile came to her lips. One day she hoped she'd be able to repay his kindness. . . .

Chapter 8

Although she was trying to enjoy herself, Catherine was having less than a good time during dinner the following Sunday. Mr. Moreau had insisted that Roberta spend the weekend with them, and he had asked Mathias to join them for the evening. Having to listen to Roberta's constant, forced gaiety was beginning to wear on Catherine's nerves. Moreover, the woman was hopelessly overdressed for the occasion. Her red, hennaed hair was worn loose to her shoulders in a style totally unbecoming to a woman in her early fifties. She was wearing a black silk hostess gown with a plunging neckline that revealed entirely too much. Her flashy diamond earrings, as well, seemed to Catherine to be completely out of place for the occasion.

"Isn't that one of the dresses we bought in Paris?" Roberta asked, leaning toward Catherine with a bright smile on her ruby red lips.

Catherine ignored the "we" and answered, "Yes, it is. This is the first time I've worn it, though."

"It's very becoming," Mathias said, reaching out his hand and taking hers. "But on you, everything is."

She glanced at him briefly, warmed by his compliment, but sensing that there was something on his mind. His blue green eyes seemed veiled this evening, as if he had a secret. "Thank you, Mathias," she said, withdrawing her hand before her father could glare at her. She knew perfectly well that the older man didn't approve of any show of affection in the company of others, and the evening was already proving difficult enough without incurring his irritation, as well.

Mrs. Campbell entered the dining room carrying a tray of assorted French pastries. She stopped at Roberta first, who threw her hands into the air like a teenage girl. "Oh, no, thank you, Mrs. Campbell. They're absolutely terrible for the hips." She turned to Mr. Moreau and gently rested her hand on his arm. "And you shouldn't eat any, either, dear. They're terribly high in cholesterol."

His gray eyes peered at her from beneath his thick-set eyebrows. "Why should I worry about cholesterol?" he said, taking a blueberry tart from the tray and putting it on his dessert plate. "I'm in good condition, and it's not as if I indulge in sweets regularly."

"Of course you are, dear, but we do want to keep you that way, don't we?" The smile never left her lips. "I understand, Mathias, that you're quite the polo player. Pierre says that you play every Sunday, is that correct?" She lifted her coffee cup with her right hand, her little finger curled daintily.

Mathias grinned proudly. "Well, not every Sunday, but as often as we can get two teams together."

"We've checked the sports pages from time to time—haven't we, dear—but we never see any mention of the game."

"It hasn't been all that popular in France in the past few years," Mathias said, "but it's making a comeback now. I'm even teaching Catherine how to ride, and she's a very good pupil."

"English saddle, of course," Roberta said.

"Of course. However, I don't think she's quite ready to tackle competitive sports."

"Do women play the game?" Mr. Moreau glanced at Mathias. "I always thought polo was strictly a man's sport."

"It is, Pierre. I wasn't thinking about polo for Catherine, for it's much too dangerous to risk her pretty head. I was thinking more of dressage competitions. She sits a horse well and seems to have a natural inclination. I'm surprised that you didn't enroll her in equitation classes when she was still a girl."

"I was away at school," Catherine put in, wishing the dinner would come to an end. "I could have taken lessons if I'd wanted to, but I was always more interested in tennis . . . until meeting you, of course."

"You're a dream come true, Catherine," he said, turning back to her. "No matter what I'm doing, you always take an immediate interest. There aren't many young women like that anymore. They all seem to be totally involved with themselves these days."

"Oh, that's nothing new," Roberta said with a musical titter. "Some women have always been quite selfish at heart."

Mathias smiled, fixing his aquamarine eyes on Roberta, who was seated across from him. "Surely you're much too young to know what women have been like historically."

"Dear boy!" she responded gleefully. "Why, I'm practically Pierre's age."

Catherine tried to hide the smile that threatened to betray her amusement. Mathias had really boxed himself into a corner. If he volunteered that Roberta didn't look like it, it would imply that Pierre appeared far older than his own age. But if he didn't respond to Roberta's confession, he risked offending her. Feeling sorry for him in the awkward situation, Catherine decided to help him out. "I think it's the superior nutrition, don't you? Fifty years ago, a person was considered old at forty. But today, one can look young and healthy as long as one wishes to."

"Well, not forever," Roberta remarked. "But I think you have a point. *Our* generation," she said, looking warmly at Pierre, "has many more benefits than our parents did. Don't you think so, dear?"

"I really wouldn't know, Roberta. Frankly, I think the modern preoccupation with eternal youth is a waste of time."

"Surely, Pierre," Roberta pressed, "you'd far prefer to be seen with someone attractive than with a frumpy, gray-haired woman!" She leaned toward Mathias and stage-whispered, "He tends to take many things for granted, Mathias."

Mr. Moreau sighed and pulled out a panatela, which he offered to Mathias. "Frankly, Roberta, as long as people don't allow themselves to become slovenly, I don't see that it matters very much how old they may look."

"Would you forgive us, Pierre?" Mathias said, declining the proffered cigar. "I'd like to take a little walk with Catherine. It's a perfect evening for it."

"I'd love that," Catherine agreed, grateful for the chance to get away from Roberta.

"Go on," Mr. Moreau said quietly. "You two young people have a nice time, and Roberta and I will be in the living room having a brandy."

As she rose from the table, Catherine didn't miss the slight grimace on Roberta's face. "I'll only be a second, Mathias," Catherine said, ignoring it. I just want to get a light sweater."

"I'll be waiting for you outside," he responded.

She ran upstairs and was just coming back down when she heard Roberta say, "He seems like a very eligible bachelor, Pierre. Do you think they'll get married?"

"I couldn't say."

"What would you do if Catherine moved away? This is a terribly large house to live in all by yourself."

"I managed when she was away at school, Roberta."

"Yes, I know, but you really should be thinking about your own future, Pierre. You're still young and you shouldn't live just for the factory. Once Catherine's married, you'll want to start thinking about your own life again. You've already given up so much for her, dear. . . ."

Catherine didn't hear the rest, but it didn't escape her that the woman was angling for her own benefit. She'd known for quite some time that Roberta would be delighted if she would marry again, and Catherine's father seemed to be the prime target. She only hoped that he had the good sense to see through her scheme and not make a serious mistake.

But once outside under the starry mantle of night, she forgot about the two of them and linked her arm through Mathias's. "What a splendid idea you had," she remarked.

"I'm quite fond of your father," he said, squeezing her hand, "but I can't abide cigars or prattling women."

She smiled. "But there are dozens of prattling women at the club you belong to."

"Maybe, but they're also married to wealth or power— I can endure anything for business. However, your aunt doesn't fit into that heading."

"She's not my aunt," Catherine protested too quickly. "That is, only by marriage. She married my father's older brother, but ever since he died about nine years ago, she's been playing the woe-is-me role to the hilt."

"She seems to have your father convinced, that's pretty obvious. Do you think he's entertaining any ideas about marrying her?"

Catherine shuddered. "I hope not! Can you imagine a lifetime of Sunday dinners listening to that shrill voice of hers?"

"No," he replied, laughing, then stopped walking and put his hands on Catherine's shoulders. "But I can easily imagine it with you."

"Please, Mathias, don't talk that way," she said softly. "You know how nervous it makes me when you start to get that serious look in your eyes."

"But why, Catherine? You know I'm crazy about you, that I want you to marry me—why do you refuse to listen?"

"I guess I'm just not ready, Mathias. I just got out of school and I haven't even begun to try my wings yet. I'd like a life of my own before I get married."

Mathias dropped his eyes. "I suppose it is a bit selfish of me. I'm ten years older than you are and have had plenty of time to sow my oats. But it drives me crazy, darling, when you're away from me. I keep wondering what you're doing, who you might be meeting."

"But we've only known each other about six weeks, Mathias. How can you be so sure you're in love with me?"

He chuckled. "I was in love with you the first time

I saw you, when you were still a teenager. I guess I just never realized it until you came back to St. Cloud this March." He turned aside for a moment. "Is it my age, Catherine? Is that what's worrying you?"

"No, of course not. I just don't think we've known each other long enough to make so serious a decision. When I get married, Mathias, I don't want to have any reservations about it. I want to be very sure I'm doing the right thing."

He took her into his arms gently, nuzzling his chin against her curly brown hair. "I'd do anything in the world for you, darling—you know that, don't you?"

She allowed herself to be held, comfortably nestled against Mathias's chest. It still amazed her that this dashing, older man found her so attractive, that he loved her so openly. When Mathias had first told her of his feelings about ten days before, she had more or less laughed it off, thinking he was just teasing. But the crushed look in his eyes told her she'd been wrong. He had meant what he said.

Catherine had never been in love before and didn't know if what she felt toward Mathias was true love or not. She enjoyed being in his company, liked being taken to so many places and meeting such interesting people, and found his attentive adoration more than merely flattering. But did she love him? She didn't know. Her father's approval of Mathias meant more to her than she would care to admit, but was that sufficient reason to marry Mathias? Again she wished fervently that her mother was still alive. A woman needs her mother's guidance in such things. Had her mother had any misgivings before marriage?

The tiny red glow of a cigarette caught Catherine's

attention suddenly, and she pulled out of Mathias's arms.

"Michael? Is that you?" she called into the darkness.

"Hello, there," the masculine voice answered.

Catherine tugged at Mathias's arm, pulling him away from the street light toward her neighbor's front yard. Mathias went along with her, although a little unwillingly. "You'll like him, Mathias," she said in a low voice "He's a newspaper reporter and very well traveled."

Seconds later she was making the introductions and the two men shook hands. "Though we haven't met formally," Michael said, "I'm a great admirer of yours."

"That's right," Catherine said. "I'd forgotten that you two have played polo against each other." She turned to Mathias and explained, "Michael plays with The Bennetts."

"The team you trounced a couple of months ago," the man in question added with a smile.

"It was a very uneven match," Mathias conceded. "We never should have been pitted against one another. You fellows need a lot more practice before you can hope to beat The Wolves."

"Well, polo's just a game for us. We're not as serious as you fellows are."

"Perhaps not, but a couple of the goals you scored were really very good. You just need to get out on the field more often," Mathias said graciously.

"Michael," Catherine interrupted, "why don't you come back with us and have some coffee or a brandy? I'm sure father would like to see you again."

"I don't think so, Catherine," Michael said. "I'm not dressed for it and I'd feel out of place."

"Don't be stubborn, Michael. No one cares how you're dressed!"

"Thanks, but some other time, perhaps. You've got company, and I can tell by what you're wearing that my showing up in cords and a sweater wouldn't sit very well with your father."

"Well, nice meeting you," Mathias said, already putting his hand under Catherine's elbow.

"Same here," Michael responded.

Catherine looked disappointed, but tried to hide it. "Were you able to get that information for me?" she asked, holding back a little.

"Not yet, Catherine. I'll need more to go on, I'm afraid. How about if I come over tomorrow morning, and you can give me some more details."

"I'll do my best," she answered. "But as you know, I don't know much more than what I've already told you."

She felt Mathias give her a light tug and, almost wistfully, she let herself be led back to her home. When they were going up the front walk, she turned to her companion quizzically. "Why were you so anxious to get away from Michael?"

He smiled down at her, putting his arm about her shoulder. "It's getting a little chilly out here for you, that's all. Andrews seems a nice enough fellow, I suppose."

"Michael's not all that young," Catherine said as they mounted the stairs. "He's twenty-five, and he's led a very exciting life already."

"Is that all? He looked much younger to me—maybe in the daylight he wouldn't. You really like him quite a bit, don't you?"

"He knows about all sorts of things, Mathias, and he's been very kind to me."

"Have you ever gone out with him? On a date, I mean?"

Catherine nodded. "A couple of times."

Unexpectedly Mathias took her by the shoulders and stared into her eyes intently. "You're not attracted to him, are you? A newspaper reporter who doesn't even bother to dress properly?"

Suddenly vexed, Catherine pulled out of his grasp. "How dare you say such a thing? And why should anyone put on a good suit just to have supper alone?"

Mathias's arms dropped to his side as they stood in front of the door. "I'm sorry, darling—I just got jealous, that's all. I really don't want you seeing any other men. Please, can't we become engaged?"

She looked into his earnest eyes, but much as she wanted to make Mathias happy, she simply couldn't agree to an engagement so quickly. "I'm not seeing Michael in that way, Mathias. You're making too much of our friendship. Even if you and I were to get married, I wouldn't stop seeing Michael. He's a sensitive and caring person, and I value his friendship. Can't a man and a woman just be friends?"

"Of course," Mathias answered, opening the door for her. "I love you so much I'm not thinking straight."

She entered the foyer, and in the light there noticed that Mathias's smile was a little forced. If he was that jealous now, she wondered what he'd be like after they were married. It was at that moment that Catherine realized she was already accepting his proposal . . . if not vocally, then in her own mind. It felt strange, as if she had lost control of her own life. What was it that Michael had said that day . . . ? That if she didn't complicate her thinking with a lot of what ifs and maybes, life wasn't that difficult.

Obviously Michael knew what he wanted and how to get it. So did Mathias for that matter. But Catherine wasn't at all sure she knew what she wanted. . . .

Chapter 9

Michael came over around nine-thirty the next morning. It was the first time Catherine had seen him in a business suit and she thought he looked very attractive. After Mathias's outburst the evening before, she found herself feeling a little uncomfortable. It had never entered her head to think of Michael as a possible suitor, nor had he done anything to indicate that he was interested in being anything but her friend.

"You're looking very dapper today," she said as they went into the living room.

"I have an interview at noon with a tycoon, so of course I have to look respectable. Want to come with me?"

She laughed lightly. "I don't think that would look too good, do you? After all, friends don't just tag along on important interviews. Will it be the feature assignment you've been hoping for?"

"That all depends on how well I write it, but my chances are pretty good. The fellow's a self-made billionaire, and he virtually controls the shipping industry. I just have to get the right slant for the story, that's all. And I'm hoping he's not a mumbler."

Catherine laughed, wishing she could go along but a little shy about accepting Michael's invitation. "Well, what else do you need to know about my mother?" she asked, getting directly to the point.

He sat down in Mr. Moreau's striped armchair. "Just exactly when did she die, Catherine? Her obituary doesn't show up on the Cardex scanner, but that doesn't mean very much. I never have trusted those computers anyhow."

"Be careful what you say," Catherine warned. Moreau Electronics supplies most of the components for them." Her smile belied the warning in her words. "Let's see, it was eleven years ago and I was away at school. It was winter, I remember, but the exact date . . . ." She raised her hands helplessly.

"Is Josephine home? Let me see if I can get some information out of her."

They left the room and went toward the kitchen, where the old woman spent much of her time in the company of Mrs. Campbell. Now that Catherine was grown, there was little for Josephine to do, so she busied herself playing the role of housekeeper—planning the menus with the cook and supervising the cleaning lady who came in twice a week.

Josephine was helping the cook peel potatoes when they entered the kitchen, and she looked up with mild surprise. Wiping her hands on the towel she had spread across her lap, she got to her feet with a twinkle in her dark brown eyes. "We have a visitor, Mrs. Campbell. The young ruffian from next door . . . Michael Andrews."

"You haven't changed a bit, Josephine," he said, grinning.

"How do you do, Mrs. Campbell?"

"Humph!" Josephine said with a chuckle. "I hope *you* have. I don't know how many times I had to chase you out of our garden when you were a lad."

Michael, towering over the old woman, seemed very pleased to see her. "You probably saved my life each time," he said, then turned to Catherine. "I was very fond of swinging by my knees from the branches of your trees—I was going through a Tarzan phase."

"Yes, and I remember the time when you fell—you nearly scared me to death!"

"He's still falling out of trees!" Catherine said, unable to resist telling about their first encounter.

They all sat down at the table, and Mrs. Campbell fixed them a pot of tea while they chatted. Later Michael asked permission to smoke in front of Josephine—a courtesy that obviously pleased her enormously—and then leaned back in his chair. "I've been toying with an idea for the paper, Josephine, and I thought you might be able to help me."

"What is it?" she asked curiously.

"The effect of parental loss on young children. I was discussing the subject with Catherine the other evening," he said, pressing his foot against hers as if to tell her she should let him handle this. "I was already well into my teens when my own folks died, but how old was Catherine?"

Josephine's eyes became clouded, an expression which Catherine knew quite well meant that the old woman had become guarded. "Eleven," Josephine answered after a moment's silence.

"Do you happen to remember the exact date? Catherine doesn't, but readers like to have the statistics in such articles."

"February 7. . . ." Josephine frowned.

Catherine could sense that she was pulling back, not at all liking the turn that the conversation had taken. Michael had managed to get information he needed, but she could tell he'd have a hard time learning anything more.

"Was it from a prolonged illness?" he asked, a friendly look in his brown eyes.

"You'll have to ask Mr. Moreau," Josephine said tightly.

"But surely you'd remember," Michael prodded innocently.

Josephine squared her shoulders. "I don't want to seem rude, Michael, but there are some things that I do not believe the household staff should discuss. If you want information about Mrs. Moreau, you'll just have to ask her husband. And he's not likely to tell you much," she added with a knowing look in Catherine's direction.

"Yes," Michael said carefully, "Catherine's already told me that he won't discuss anything about his wife . . . that's why I thought you might help me out."

"I'd like to, Michael, please believe that. But I'm a salaried employee in this household . . . who should have been discharged years ago. It's only because Mr. Moreau is a good man that I haven't been put out to pasture. He knows perfectly well that I'd have nowhere to go if I left here, and I appreciate his compassion."

"How could he fire you?" Catherine asked, shocked. "You're as much a part of this household as he or I."

"Why do you always think the worst of him, child? Of course he could discharge me if he wanted to . . . I don't have a contract. But your father has granted me permission to live in this house until the day I die, and I owe him a great deal for that.''

Catherine shook her head, confused. "Maybe it's because I don't *know* him, Josephine. He never confides in me and he never has. All these years, whenever I've mentioned mother or wanted to know something about her, he's acted as if I'd just plunged an ice pick into his heart. He has always resented me and . . . .''

"Hush up, Catherine! I won't have you speaking that way! I raised your father and I know him very well. But it is not for me to discuss him or his decisions with anyone. He . . . well, he missed your mother, child. And you look so very much like her that sometimes I think it's very painful for him. Now, that's as much as I care to say.''

Catherine smiled ruefully. "She's got that look on her face, Michael . . . Josephine means it.''

Michael nodded. "Well, maybe it wasn't such a good story idea after all." He pushed back the wooden chair and got to his feet. "It was very nice seeing you again, Josephine. Whenever you feel like it, I'd be happy if you'd come to visit me. I can't bake cookies as good as Mrs. Campbell's, but I don't think you'll choke on mine. Will you drop in sometime?''

"I'd be happy to, Michael. I haven't set foot in your house since . . . .''

"No one has," he interrupted gently. "Except Catherine, of course.''

"I've noticed you don't have many visitors," the old woman said, her earlier cheer fully restored.

"I'm a private man, Josephine. I like my solitude, and since my work brings me into so much contact with people, I'm only alone when I'm at home. But I'll make an exception for you," he added, going over to her and bending down to give her a hug. "I promise to be a gentleman when you come over," he teased.

Her smile was genuinely amused. "As I'm sure you'd want to be around a woman my age!"

"You still have a very well-turned ankle, I've noticed."

"And I can still chase you across the yard if I have to. Go on, now, both of you! Go waste someone else's time."

As they left the kitchen, they overheard Mrs. Campbell saying, "I think my ankles are nicer than yours, actually."

Catherine and Michael exchanged a smile, then broke into laughter as they crossed the dining room. They reached the double doors leading to the living room, and she paused. "Michael?" she said.

"Hmm?"

"Would you come up to the attic with me? I think I remember a long time ago Josephine mentioning that father put all the pictures of my mother there. . . ."

"Sure, I'll come up with you. Who knows, there may be things that go bump in the night and I'll be able to protect you!" He removed his jacket and tie and draped them over the bench in the foyer. "I can't risk getting them dusty before my appointment," he explained.

She led him to the back of the house where a narrow staircase rose steeply behind a door.

"Do you want to hold my hand?" he asked in a somber whisper.

"No, silly, we'd never fit on the stairs!" she giggled.

They climbed up the rough wooden steps until they reached the third floor. Part of that floor had been servants' quarters in the past, though only Josephine had lived up there for as long as Catherine could remember. Sealed off from that section and taking up most of the space was the attic.

Catherine opened the door and glanced around, taking in the cartons and trunks, the drape cloths over bulky items of furniture. "I haven't been up here since I was a little girl," she said softly, trying to remember if it had always been so crowded.

Michael started peering under the white cloths. "Seems to be a complete bedroom set over here," he said.

"Let me see," she said, moving to where he stood. The moment she saw the carved headboard, memory flooded back. "I remember that set," she said, taken aback. "It used to be in their bedroom."

"Your parents'?"

She nodded. "When I was little, too young to go to school, I used to climb into bed with them on Sundays, and mother would read the funnies to me. It used to annoy father sometimes, so we'd sneak downstairs and have a roll and milk together—at least I did; I daresay mother had coffee."

"I wonder why it was moved up here?"

Catherine shook her head. "Maybe father found it too painful a reminder after mother died."

"That's probably it," Michael concurred. "But you'd think he'd sell it or give it away if that was the case. Does he ever come up here?"

"No, not that I know of." She watched as Michael rummaged through some other things, then started looking around herself. Several rectangular objects were stacked against one wall and even though they were covered, they looked as if they might be large framed pictures or paintings. Picking her way over to them, Catherine lifted a corner of one covering. A beautifully framed gravure showed a stiffly posed couple wearing turn-of-the-century clothing.

Michael joined her and bent down to see better. "Who are they?"

"My grandparents, I think. I never met them. Don't they look austere, though?"

"I'll say. What's this one?" he asked, removing the cover from a tall frame at the back of the pile. "It's your mother!"

Catherine watched as he lifted out the portrait in oils that she had remembered hanging in her father's den. She gasped at the lifelike rendering, feeling as if she were looking into a mirror. Her mother's hairstyle was now quite out of date, but the dress wasn't. It was a formal, soft blue gown, designed in a style worn by the women of classical Greece. At the bodice, a lovely antique cameo in a gold frame seemed to be holding the fabric chastely together. "I remember that brooch," she whispered to herself.

"I do, too," Michael said. "She used to wear it frequently. I can recall asking her one day where she had got it, and she said, 'It was a gift of love!' That always struck me as wonderfully romantic and poetic." Michael laughed under his breath. "It's funny how little things come back to you, even years later."

"Maybe father gave it to her."

"That sounds like a pretty safe bet," Michael remarked. "C'mon, let's see what else is up here. Shall I put the painting back?"

"No, I want to take it down to my room."

"Isn't that kind of risky? What if your father should go into your room?"

"He never does . . . why should he now? But I won't hang it on my wall, just in case."

They began to examine boxes, whose contents were neatly labeled on the sides of most of them. Bits of dust danced in the shafts of sunlight from the dormer windows, but otherwise the attic was remarkably clean. Finally they reached a trunk and Michael opened the lid. Inside were several photo albums. Catherine carefully removed the one on top and slowly turned the pages. There were snapshots of her parents at the beach, laughing, and another that showed her parents throwing snowballs at another couple. In this last one, Catherine didn't recognize the man at all, but after a few moments she realized that the woman was Roberta. How young and carefree they all seemed! It was almost a shock for her to see her father having such a good time. Obviously the man her mother had married had been very different from the man Catherine had grown up around. He had been very tall and lean back then, with a rather boyish, shy quality about him.

But her mother was exactly what Catherine had expected. A warm and fun-loving disposition radiated through the pictures, in total contrast to the formality of the oil painting. A sense of loss coursed through Catherine as she continued to turn the album's pages. There was a picture showing Mr. Moreau holding her as an infant; another of Catherine teetering on her first tricycle. . . . It must have been a time of happiness and security, of family unity and optimism. How different life had been since her mother had died.

"Have you seen enough?" Michael asked.

She had almost forgotten that he was there and was startled by his voice. "I think Josephine purposefully left these accessible," she replied quietly. "I'm sure she could have locked this trunk and everything else."

"What makes you think so?"

Catherine shrugged. "Just a hunch, that's all. For years I've sensed that she must have made my father a promise of some kind. Maybe he forbade her to discuss my mother with me. But as far as I know, the door to the attic has never been locked, nor has she ever told me that I couldn't come up here."

"That could be sheer coincidence," he said.

"Well, yes, of course it might be. But I don't think it is. I think she knew of my curiosity and how much I miss mother. I believe Josephine wanted me to find these albums, to get some idea of what mother was like without my having to ask questions she couldn't answer."

"You may be right at that," he said.

"Help me carry these things down to my room, will you, Michael?"

"You're really all that confident that your dad won't go into your room?"

"Yes."

"But what if he should come up here, wanting to look at all this—and then find it's missing?"

"It's a chance I'll have to take," she answered simply.

"Wouldn't it be wiser, Catherine, to leave these things here and just slip back up whenever you want to look at them?"

"Probably," she agreed. "But I want them where I can look at them anytime. Once I've had a chance to see them all, really get a feeling of what mother was like, then maybe I'll bring them back up here. I've lived the last eleven years wondering what she was like, Michael . . . and this is the first clue about her I've had."

Silently he took the photo albums from the trunk and lifted the oil painting under his arm. "I'm not sure about this, Catherine, but I can understand how you feel. C'mon, let's get it over with before we run head-on into your father. I feel like a thief."

"No," she contradicted. "We're not stealing any-thing. It's me who was robbed!"

Chapter 10

Over the next few weeks Catherine existed in a delirious spin of social engagements, all with Mathias. She saw him almost every evening; he took her to plays, to the ballet, to operas, and he introduced her to ever increasing numbers of his friends. Most of them seemed happy to meet her and treated her as if she were one of their set.

On weekends they went for long drives in the country and Mathias would patiently stop the car whenever she'd ask him so that she could take a particular photograph. As it grew warmer they were invited to lawn parties, and whenever possible, Mathias continued to play polo on Sundays. By then Catherine knew just about all The Wolves fans who attended the games, all of whom—to one degree or another—accepted her into their circle.

She had also seen Michael several times, but only because, as neighbors, they had happened across each other from time to time. They had taken a long walk one afternoon, discussing poetry and music . . . and, of course, his work. Catherine had shown him a copy of the printed annual report, and Michael had been impressed, congratulating her for the fine job she had done.

Indeed, he had responded more than her own father had, for when Mr. Moreau had seen the finished product, he had merely grunted, "I hope the rewards justify the expense."

Mathias, fortunately, had told her of the favorable comments they had been receiving from shareholders and how the sale of stocks had increased as well.

One afternoon Catherine had asked Michael if he had been able to find out any more information about where her mother was buried. He had merely shaken his head. "Not yet. It seems to be the best-kept secret in Paris, but I'm still working on it."

Later that same day, it had suddenly occurred to her that perhaps their parish minister might know. After all, she figured, there must have been a service of some kind. Yet when she'd dropped by to see Reverend Colbert he had been somewhat taciturn. "Your father never gave me any valid reasons," the man had said, "only that he didn't wish to have your mother buried in the parish graveyard and that there was to be no service. He didn't even tell me in person, but telephoned instead. I thought it very strange at the time, but then I figured that he was probably having the body cremated."

Catherine had been unprepared for that possibility and it must have shown on her face.

"Oh, yes, Miss Moreau, that thought was uppermost in my mind. It was the only possible reason I could think of as to why your mother wouldn't be buried here. She was a good woman, you know. Everyone liked her. She used to help out whenever we had fund-raising projects for charities, and she came to services regularly.''

When Catherine had left the rectory, her disappointment was mingled with confusion. While she knew her father wasn't exactly a devout churchgoer, she had never known him to buck tradition. There had never been any question that she herself wouldn't have a church wedding. And it was inconceivable to Catherine that he might have had her mother cremated! But on the other hand, it might well explain why Michael was having so much trouble finding any records. Perhaps her father hadn't informed anyone other than the coroner's office of his wife's death, knowing that there would be a considerable amount of adverse gossip if it were known he'd requested the woman's body to be disposed of in that manner. And he would certainly not have wanted anyone in the parish to know anything about it!

She decided that the best thing to do was to let Michael continue delving into the mystery and to see what he could come up with. But she decided to tell him about her visit to Reverend Colbert and what the man suspected. Perhaps Michael could check the records with the coroner's office, for there was no way her father could have concealed the information from them!

She had very little time to think about such things, however, during those few weeks. She lived in a constant whirl of activity and, because she was still quite unaccustomed to doing so, the days and evenings seemed to whiz by in a flurry of excitement. Once again Mr. Moreau insisted that she allow Roberta to accompany her on a shopping spree to buy formal clothes for the summer months. This time, Catherine didn't protest. It was now all too obvious to her that to be with Mathias, she needed an extensive wardrobe, for most of the women in his circle of friends were never seen in the same gown twice. It was fashionable to go to the opera in formal attire, then later to have supper at Maxim's or another extravagant Paris restaurant.

People were beginning to recognize her now and to treat her as part of an elite corps of socialites; even the maitre d's in many restaurants knew who she was and were most deferential. It was like living in a movie, surrounded by influential and beautiful people, and Catherine was dazzled by it.

Yet, during the weekdays when her father was at the factory, Catherine would frequently take out the photo albums she had found in the attic and would study the pictures of her mother carefully. Though she had known that Roberta had been involved in the family for a number of years, she had never realized how much her parents had socialized with her and her husband. It seemed as if the two couples had been inseparable companions; but since the snapshots weren't dated, it was impossible to tell what time span they covered.

On the Thursday of the second week in July, her father had phoned her from his office. "Catherine, will you be home this evening?" he had asked.

"It's somewhat tentative, father. Mathias said he might have a business appointment tonight, but that he'd call me this afternoon to let me know for sure."

"A business appointment?" There was a brief pause as if the information had surprised him. "I would appreciate it, Catherine, if you would arrange to be home this evening. I wish to have a talk with you."

Automatically she tried to remember if there had been anything she had done that might have offended him. "Certainly, father, if you wish. If Mathias can be unsure of his plans, then I'm entitled to make other arrangements. Was there something in particular you wanted to discuss?" She felt like a little girl again, being told to go to her room until he could come upstairs and scold her for some infraction she'd committed.

"It will keep until I see you later," he replied, and then abruptly said goodbye and hung up.

His phone call had all but ruined the rest of her afternoon, and she impatiently waited for evening. Whatever he wanted to talk about, she wanted it over with and out of the way. By six o'clock Catherine was at the living-room window, watching for her father's sedan to pull up.

"You're as nervous as a cat this afternoon, child," Josephine said, bringing in a silver bowl heaped with ice cubes. "I don't think you're getting enough rest."

"I am a little tired," she admitted reluctantly, "but it's just because I'm not accustomed to all this nightlife. I marvel at Mathias, who can stay up until one or two in the morning, then go to work the next day."

"Perhaps he has a stronger constitution than you do, child. Does he have to keep you out so late?"

Catherine lifted her shoulders slightly. "Well, the theaters don't get out until eleven or eleven-thirty, then it's off for supper. Invariably we run into friends who insist we have a nightcap with them . . . and one thing leads to another. It's just impossible to get home sooner."

"I don't like it, Catherine. You've never been so frivolous before. . . . I hardly recognize you these days."

"Oh, Josephine," Catherine said, going over and

putting her arms around the old woman. "It won't last much longer, I'm sure. As a matter of fact, I'm staying home tonight."

"For a change," Josephine grumbled.

"Don't begrudge me a little fun. I'm young and I'm having a wonderful time. Mathias treats me like a queen, and I'm going out to all sorts of places I've never been to before."

"Well, I'm glad he shows you the proper respect, but I'd like it better if he would manage to get you home at a decent hour. You could have something to eat before the theater, couldn't you?"

"I suppose so, but no one else ever seems to. It's like a game we all know the rules of. You catch a show and then meet with your friends and talk about what's new. The Kemmerings, a nice couple I've met through Mathias, are always on the go. They're leaving for Brazil next week. Isn't that fascinating? I can't wait till they get back so I can hear all about it"

"Brazil at this time of year?"

"The seasons are reversed below the equator," she explained. "But just imagine it, Josephine. In Paris one moment, then in romantic Rio de Janeiro the next!"

Josephine shook her head. "I've never understood this craving to be constantly going places. What's wrong with staying at home?"

"Nothing's wrong with it," Catherine laughed. "But it's exciting to see new places and learn about different styles of life."

"Only if you're bored with what you have. And bored people have no inner reserves. That's why they have to keep going out and keeping busy—because there's nothing inside," she concluded, pointing an arthritic finger at her temple. "You used to read a great deal, child."

"I was in school," Catherine explained lamely, knowing perfectly well that the old woman was right. What was worse, she had even stopped reading the newspapers that she had begun to read as a habit shortly after meeting Michael.

"And you were going to get a job as soon as you felt well enough," Josephine pursued.

"I'm still going to," Catherine responded. "But I have plenty of time for that, Josephine. It's not as if the rent won't be paid just because I'm having fun."

The aged governess's dark eyes studied Catherine for a second. "And what about your self-respect?" she asked softly.

Catherine laughed again. "Is it in jeopardy?"

"It will be if you don't snap out of this pattern you're in. There's more to working than just earning a living, you know. A person has to feel that he's contributing to society, that he has a right to take up space on this earth. As it is, you're practically a freeloader, living off your father and adding nothing of your own that's meaningful to the world."

Catherine didn't know what to say. She was hurt and angry that Josephine should accuse her of such a thing. But then, Catherine reminded herself, Josephine had never been out in the real world. She had lived with the Moreaus for almost fifty years and had never seen any other way of life. How could she possibly know that there were other ways of looking at things? But was she rationalizing her behavior?

"I'll get a job soon, Josephine. I promise," she said quietly.

The woman snorted. "By the time you get out of bed, the day's half over."

"It's Mathias, isn't it?" Catherine said, realization dawning on her. "You resent him."

"No, that's too strong a word. But I don't like what being in his company is doing to you, Catherine. I don't know if that's his fault or yours, but you're not the girl you used to be . . . and I'm worried about you."

She softened at once. "Please don't worry, Josephine. It's just that all this is new to me. It'll wear off in a while, and then I'll knuckle down again."

"We'll see," Josephine said, pulling herself up as straight as she could. "In the meantime, I think your father's just come home."

Catherine ran to the window and saw his car pulling into the garage. Wanting to please him, she fixed his highball so it would be ready the moment he came in the door.

"I WANT TO TALK to you about Mathias," Mr. Moreau said, seating himself in his favorite chair, his drink at his elbow, and lighting up a cigar.

Catherine had curled up on the brown sofa across from him, a perplexed expression on her face. Was he too going to lecture her about her life?

"You may think me an old-fashioned man, Catherine, but I've been concerned about you lately. It has reached the point where I'm being asked by people if I'm related to you, as if you were some kind of celebrity."

She bit back her amusement. "That's only because Mathias is important in the social pages," she replied.

"A fact which I had been ignorant of until lately. But

that isn't the point. I had lunch with Mathias today, Catherine, and I asked him what his intentions are."

"His intentions? But he can't stop the photographers, father."

"That's not what I mean. As your father, I have a right to know what your relationship with Mathias is going to lead to. You're not seeing anyone else—to my knowledge—and if he's going to monopolize your time, then I have to know where this may lead."

"You didn't ask him, father! That sort of thing went out with high-button shoes!" Catherine suddenly felt humiliated and wondered how poor Mathias had taken the luncheon interrogation.

"Perhaps it has 'gone out,' Catherine, but that doesn't mean it wasn't a good practice. I am responsible for your future, even though you are past twenty-one and particularly since you are living under my roof."

She sighed and resigned herself to what would surely follow: that she wasn't supposed to see Mathias anymore.

"Actually, I was rather surprised at the way Mathias reacted to my questions."

"Oh?"

Mr. Moreau nodded solemnly. "He said that he has asked you to marry him repeatedly, but that you always put him off with some excuse—usually that you want your own career first. Is that correct, Catherine?"

"Close enough," she responded.

"He made it abundantly clear that he is seriously in love with you and that he wants you to be his wife. Fortunately, we didn't have to go into his prospects since I know perfectly well what his future can be if he stays with the company."

"He enjoys his work, father, and obviously you pay him handsomely."

"Why do you say that?" His gray eyes squinted at her from over the rim of his glass.

"Well, his sports car, his clothes, the fact that he can afford to take me to so many expensive places . . . ."

Mr. Moreau shook his head slowly. "Mathias earns a respectable salary for the kind of work he does, Catherine. But not enough to live in his chosen manner, which is another thing I asked him about. It seems that he has a trust fund from a deceased aunt or something. He explained it to me today, but I forget now how close the relationship was. I have always found it curious that he spends money so lavishly, but before he became involved with you, it was none of my business. Now, of course, I feel entitled to know how he manages on his salary."

Catherine closed her dark blue eyes tightly before responding. "He must have been terribly embarrassed, father. How could you have asked him something so personal?"

"He took it very well, as I expected him to. His manner was direct and forthright, and he agreed that a father is correct in wanting to more about his future son-in-law."

"But I haven't agreed to marry him!"

"I realize that, Catherine, and that's why I wished to speak with you. Why have you not accepted his proposal?"

She looked past him to the mantel above the fireplace, trying to find a suitable explanation. In truth, she didn't have one. "I just think it's too soon for me to get married," she answered lamely.

"While I'm glad you're not rushing into things, aren't

you forgetting that engagements were designed to give a couple some time to get to know each other before taking their vows?"

"Maybe you're right," she conceded with a little smile. "It's just that Mathias seems to pressure me so urgently. . . . I suppose I've felt rushed."

"Do you love him, Catherine?"

She stood up and went over to the windows that overlooked the front lawn. "I'm not sure," she answered softly. "I've never dated anyone like him before, father. He's handsome and we have a great deal of fun together, but I don't know if that's love." Catherine had been about to add how much she wished her mother were still alive, but she caught herself in time.

"Don't you have any close female friends who could counsel you about this?"

"It's such a personal thing, father. I don't know any women to whom I'd confide such things."

"Then I recommend that you telephone your Aunt Roberta and arrange to see her. I'm sure she would be most pleased to be of help to you."

"Roberta! No, father, thank you very much, but no . . . not Roberta."

Her father set his glass down on the table beside him and took a deep breath. "Then you must make up your mind in some other way, Catherine. You will soon be twenty-three. Either tell Mathias point-blank that you will not be marrying him or accept his proposal. If it's a career you want first, then you should be getting on with it. As it is, however, you're accomplishing nothing, and it's very unfair to Mathias."

Again, with her father's words, she felt the pangs of rejection. He didn't care what her feelings were as much as how her existence was affecting his employee. "I take it, father, that you want me to marry him," she said tonelessly.

"I believe it would be a highly suitable arrangement. I've taken a greater interest in Mathias since the two of you have been seeing so much of each other, and I find him a very solid young man. You could do far worse. Besides, love isn't everything. Compatibility, similar interests—these are the things that make a marriage work. Love can wear off and leave you with a ruined life."

His voice sounded so hollow at the end of his statement that Catherine turned around and looked at him. Had the love between him and her mother faded? Was that why he was such an embittered man? She didn't know, but she felt she had had a tiny glimpse of something within him that she had never seen before.

Mr. Moreau rose from his chair as the soft tinkle of a bell announced that dinner was ready. "I expect you to give Mathias your decision by the end of next week, Catherine."

"Yes, father. I will," she said, walking with him toward the dining room. Yet before they had reached the table, Catherine realized there *was* someone she could talk to, someone who could help her. Michael!

Chapter 11

She had gone over to Michael's house the following afternoon, but had found no one home. She tried calling him over the weekend, but finally gave up, figuring that he was probably out of town on an assignment. It had been such an active weekend however—even more so than usual—that Catherine had in truth scarcely had time to try to reach Michael.

Mathias had taken her to Enghien-les-Bains on Saturday for the races, and then on Sunday—unable to round up another polo team—they had gone to Meaux for the entire day, walking through the cathedral there, sightseeing, and going boating in the late afternoon. That same evening, flushed from all their outdoor activity, they stopped at a lovely restaurant on the way back and Mathias teased her about getting so much sun that she look like a tourist. Because of her tawny coloring, Catherine's skin absorbed the sun's rays immediately and she tanned easily.

Throughout the weekend she had kept trying to look at Mathias as someone she might spend the rest of her life with. There was no question that he was charming and that he possessed an easy, captivating grace. She had seen how every woman he knew flirted with him outrageously. He was a superb dancer, he liked to live very well . . . and he truly did love her. He had been a perfect gentleman over the almost four months they'd been spending in each other's company, though he had made it unavoidably clear that he would prefer it otherwise. Nonetheless, when she was in his embrace and permitting his ardent kisses, he always stopped the moment she requested it. On several occasions she had actually wondered about this. If she really loved him, would she want him to stop? During the few times when they hadn't seen one another for a few days, she had missed him . . . but not desperately. Didn't being in love mean it was unbearable to be separated?

"A penny for your thoughts," Mathias said, his blue green eyes glowing in the candlelight. He lifted his glass of wine and silently toasted her.

"Oh, nothing really," she said, not wanting to reveal what she'd been thinking. "I understand you had an awkward lunch with my father last Thursday."

"He told you? I'm surprised. I didn't think he would."

"Is that why you said nothing? Out of respect for him?"

"No, not particularly," he replied candidly. "I pretty much forgot about it, that's all. It was a lot of old world stuff, and not really worth repeating. He can be awfully stuffy sometimes."

"I know," she remarked dryly. "He wants me to marry you, Mathias."

"I'm delighted to hear that," he said, grinning. "I obviously did a good job of selling the idea, then."

"Is that what it means to you? A sales pitch?"

"Don't be touchy, darling. Obviously, I'm getting

nowhere with you, so I took advantage of your father's interest to try to convince him I was the right man for you. What's wrong with that?"

"Oh, nothing, I suppose," she said, feeling vaguely displeased. "If we were to get married, how would you feel about my having a job?"

"But you wouldn't need one, darling! I make more than enough money for us to live on—unless your father fires me, that is. But even if he did, I could always get another job."

Catherine shook her head slowly. "I wouldn't work for the money, Mathias, as much as to have a sense of my own identity."

"Well," he drawled amiably, "we can always discuss that later on. You may find you'll want to stay home and run things. It's a full-time career of its own, Catherine. If you had a job, we'd have to hire a housekeeper to do what you could be doing."

"You just said that money was no problem," Catherine reminded him gently.

"Look, I earn a fair wage at Moreau Electronics, but I don't see any point in squandering it. The way prices are soaring, even an executive wage isn't really all that much."

"But your car cost you a fortune, Mathias! You'd spend a year's salary for a vehicle and then refuse to let me pursue the career I've been trained for?"

"Don't jump to conclusions, darling," he said, his hand quickly covering hers. "For one thing, I didn't pay cash for my car. For another, you know as well as I do how important it is for me to look well-off. Hanging around with the crowd we do, we have to show a bit of class! That's just good business, Catherine."

"Well, with a combined income, we could afford a live-in housekeeper, and that shows class, too." She said it firmly, but with a light tone. "Besides, father says you have a trust fund . . . so that's three incomes."

"Ahh, yes, from my dead uncle. But it's not really a trust fund the way you mean it. My uncle had a number of investments, and, uh, well, I'm the sole heir to the dividends they pay. As you can see, dividends fluctuate, so it's not a dependable, steady income. Mind you, we wouldn't have to worry about ending up on welfare or anything, but still—"

"And your clothes are also bought on credit, then?"

Mathias laughed a little tightly. "Why am I getting the third degree, darling? You've never been interested in such things before."

She took a sip of her wine and thought over his question. "Probably because my father has insisted that I make up my mind about us. I'm feeling pushed from all sides. Besides, if I do agree to marry you, aren't I entitled to know what your financial circumstances are?"

"Once you agree, Catherine, then yes. But until then, not really. After all, I'm not asking you how much of a dowry you'll have."

She had to laugh. He was right, of course, and she was being rude to press him about such things.

"However," Mathias said, reaching into the inside pocket of his blazer, "I have a little gift that might put your mind at rest."

When Catherine saw the long, narrow velvet case, she knew at once it could only be jewelry. She watched Mathias open it and remove a stunning gold necklace with a pendant of diamonds hanging from it. In the candlelight it shimmered brilliantly, almost like a living thing. "For . . . me . . .?"

"Because I love you, Catherine. I've tried telling you and I've done everything I can to show you—perhaps this little gift will convince you." He stood up then, and came around behind her, clasping the necklace around her throat.

She automatically touched it, longing to see how it looked, yet as Mathias sat down across from her again, she couldn't think of a thing to say for a moment.

"It's perfect for you, Catherine. I knew it would be."

"But don't you think it's too extravagant?" she asked, still fingering the cluster of stones disbelievingly.

"Not for anyone as beautiful and wonderful as you," he said. "Now, not another word. I want you to have it, darling, and that's all there is to it. Shall I order for us now?" His hand raised to catch the waiter's eye and then he lifted the menu to the flickering light.

SHE AWKENED THE NEXT DAY to the harsh sounds of hammering, and wondered what time it was. *It has to be dawn*, she thought, throwing back the light coverlet and getting to her feet to go to the window. Below, as she had suspected, Michael was in his backyard repairing the wooden gate. "Have you no respect?" she shouted over the racket.

He looked up and smiled wickedly. "A respectable person would have been up hours ago! Hi, how have you been?"

"Fine," she called down, unable to be angry with him. "The real question, though, is where have *you* been?"

"In and out. I've dropped over a couple of times to see if you were in, but Josephine said you're almost never home in the evenings anymore. So she and I have had a few visits without you," he said.

"She didn't mention them," Catherine said, her brow wrinkled slightly in a frown. But then she remembered that Josephine was displeased with her at the moment and that the woman wasn't likely to share such information willingly when she was in such a mood. "Will you have some time this morning?" she called down.

"Morning's almost over, Catherine. Why? Did you want to come over?"

She nodded. "I'd like to talk to you about something, if you don't mind."

He glanced at his wristwatch quickly. "How about around one? I'll finish fixing this, make a few phone calls, and see you then, okay?"

"Fine," she called, then ducked her head back inside.

She bathed leisurely and by the time she was dressed it was already past noon. The necklace Mathias had given her the evening before was laid out on her bureau, glittering in the sunlight. Though she fully appreciated its value, the more Catherine looked at it, the more she realized it was not something she would ever have selected for herself. It was too modern and a little too flashy for her tastes. But it had been sweet of Mathias to give it to her, and she supposed that if she wore it only with very simple clothes, it might look all right.

She touched the necklace, smiled to herself, then went downstairs. "Good morning, Josephine," she said cheerily.

"Past morning, child," the old woman replied sourly, looking up from her lunch. "Mrs. Campbell had a doctor's appointment, so if you want something to eat, you'll have to fix it yourself."

Catherine ignored the chilliness in her voice. "Then I'll beg a cup of coffee from Michael," she said, reaching into the refrigerator for something to munch on.

"I heard you yelling down to him," Josephine said, blowing at the mug of hot soup on the table in front of her. "You two aren't children anymore, Catherine. Why don't you telephone him when you want to say something?"

"Because he was hammering outside and he wouldn't have heard the phone indoors," she answered, laughing. "What's the matter, Josephine? Did you get up on the wrong side of the bed this morning?"

"At least I got up," was the reply. "Maybe I'm getting old," Josephine continued, "but I just don't understand the change that's come over you."

Catherine sat down opposite Josephine and searched the woman's wrinkled face. "I promised it wouldn't be for much longer, didn't I? Please don't act as if I were committing a crime, Josephine. Even if you did something that I didn't totally approve of, I wouldn't stop loving you and I wouldn't be cold toward you."

Josephine's dark eyes looked directly at Catherine. Defensive at first, in seconds they had softened, and gradually she smiled. "You're right. And I'm sorry. I love you as if you were my very own granddaughter, child, and I guess I'm being overly protective."

Smiling, Catherine got up and went around the table to her, kissing Josephine loudly on the cheek. "Forgotten," she said. Then, glancing at the clock she added, "I'll be gone about an hour, maybe. See you later."

"If Mr. Brunton phones, what should I say?"

"The truth . . . that I'm next door having coffee. But

I doubt that he'll call. He had a business luncheon today." With that, she waved and went out the back door, careful not to let it slam. She crossed the lawn, climbed over the wall, and let herself into Michael's dining room. "Hello?"

"I'm in the living room," he called back.

She strolled toward the archway that led into the living room. "Hi," she said, and then stopped in her tracks. "When did you get all this done?" She turned to survey the completely redecorated room.

"Like it?" Michael was standing on a footstool, measuring the distance from the ceiling to the spot where he planned to hang a painting that he had temporarily rested on the floor.

"I think it's fantastic," she exclaimed genuinely. Having removed the striped wallpaper, he had painted the room a caramel color, with the molding in contrasting white enamel. The overstuffed sofas had been removed and in their place was an eye-pleasing mixture of antique and simple modern furniture. The figurines were gone and had been replaced with carved ornaments and small sculptures, which she presumed he had collected during his travels. Oriental teak bookcases flanked the large fireplace and lent a quiet elegance to the whole room. "You've done a magnificent job, Michael. It has grace and charm, yet a sense of the present and the future, as well. I would never have dared mix the periods the way you have . . . it just wouldn't have occurred to me."

"Thanks," he said, marking an X on the wall with a pencil. He took the hammer out of his hip pocket and drove in a nail with three sharp raps, then leaned down and picked up the painting. "I just bought this the other day—I think it goes well in here, don't you?"

She moved closer to him as he hung it up and leveled it. "It's very interesting; a primitive, isn't it?"

"Not really. The artist is a Mexican named Pisano. I especially like his use of colors." Then he got down from the ladder and smiled at her. "You're looking very lovely today."

"Thank you, kind sir." She pretended to curtsy, holding an imaginary skirt. "But I still think you're wonderful to have got all this done in so little time."

"Oh, you should see the upstairs—it's completely redone. Knowing myself rather well, I figured I had better start with the rooms no one ever sees. Otherwise, if I began downstairs, I'd be liable to let the second floor go. I'd get used to it and never get around to fixing it up."

"But you're away so much of the time," she said, shaking her head.

"Well, as my father used to say, people manage to get done what they want to. I figured that as long as I'm going to live here, the place should reflect my own tastes rather than my parents'. Want some coffee?"

"I'd love some," she replied, following him out of the living room and into the kitchen.

"Now then," he said, pouring out two cups from the coffee pot, "what can I do for you? Is it about your mother?"

Catherine felt suddenly shy and a little uncomfortable. "No . . . it isn't. I know you'll tell me about her as soon as you get some information."

"So what's on your mind?" He stirred his coffee and his large brown eyes took her in with warm curiosity. "C'mon, out with it."

She tried to smile but then her face became serious. "Could you be a big brother for a little while, Michael?"

"Oh, it's important, I see."

"And a little embarrassing."

He nodded and became instantly serious himself. "Big brother, priest, concerned neighbor, or just a guy who cares about you—take your pick."

She took a deep breath, then blurted out, "Have you ever been in love, Michael?"

His lips parted in a smile. "Yes, twice."

"Can you describe what it feels like?"

He leaned back in his chair, raising his eyebrows as he searched for the right answer. "Insanity. Yes, I guess that's about as close as I can get to describe what it's like. You're on top of the world when you're together, hardly able to believe your good luck; and you're miserable and despondent when you're apart. In between, there are the arguments, the delights, and the total immersion of yourself into another person's thoughts and feelings. At least, that's how it feels to me. I don't know if women love in the same way or not."

"Didn't the women you loved ever tell you how they felt about you?" she asked, bewildered.

"No," Michael answered quietly.

Catherine sighed. "I guess that's why you didn't marry either one."

"Maybe," he said cryptically. "But my own love life isn't the problem right now. Obviously you think you're in love with someone but you aren't sure."

She laced her fingers around her cup, nodding. "Mathias, this fellow I've been dating, keeps asking me to marry him . . . and my father thinks I should marry him, too."

"And how do you feel about it?" he asked gently.

"I don't know, Michael. I realize that Mathias is a

good catch, as the phrase goes, and he does have many wonderful qualities about him. But I don't feel any great surges of emotion toward him—or insanity, as you call it. No butterflies, no tingles when he kisses me . . . ."

Michael stood up and refilled his cup, though it had been only half empty. For a few moments he stood with his back to her, and Catherine knew that he must be trying to figure out how to advise her carefully. When he came back and sat down, she was vaguely surprised to notice that his eyes had an almost sad look in them.

"Why are you letting other people rush you, Catherine? You're not under any deadlines, so if you're not certain about marrying Mathias, take your time and decide for yourself."

She shook her head. "It's not that easy. Father wants me either to become engaged to Mathias or to cut off the relationship by this coming Friday."

"That's part of the trouble with living at home, Catherine. Even the most well-meaning parents can't seem to stop trying to control the lives of their children."

"Even if I moved out tomorrow and got a job immediately, that wouldn't solve anything."

"It might," Michael said slowly. "After all, you'd have some outside interests. These past four months have been very insular for you, Catherine. You're not getting any real feedback, especially since this fellow seems to be monopolizing your time. If he loves you all that much, he'll wait for you."

His tone was so positive that Catherine wondered how long Michael had waited when he had been in love. It was hard for her to imagine Michael with a woman. Other than that time when they'd gone to the

Left Bank to visit with his friends, she'd never seen Michael with other people. Even then, his friends had been a married couple, so it hadn't been the same as seeing him with a date or with the woman he loved.

She was suddenly aware that he was staring at her, and she smiled feebly. "I feel so foolish," she admitted.

"You shouldn't. Marriage is a very big step, and you should know in your heart that it's the right thing. But in all fairness, Catherine, maybe you would fall in love differently than me. There are quiet loves, too—the comfortable feeling of security and having similar interests. Many people prefer that kind of marriage."

"That's what father said, too. But I'm not so sure. . . ."

"Catherine, life is not a romantic novel. It's real. If Mathias was out of work and couldn't support you; if the children were hungry and needed shoes, but the creditors were pounding at the door, if you became seriously ill, or if he did—is he still the man you'd want to spend the rest of your life with?"

"I can't imagine Mathias in those circumstances," she said, laughing a little uncertainly.

"But it should be part of your decision, Catherine. His world is all very glamorous to you now, but what if the curtain came down on his play, and you had to see him humbled if not broken? Is he the kind of fellow who'd take any job just to be sure that you're warm? Would he fall apart or would he fight back? Can he find a sense of humor even when something has gone wrong, or does he become morose or agitated?"

"I don't know," she replied, shaking her head as if she didn't have the truth that Michael was trying to squeeze out of her.

"Look, Catherine, I'm trying to help you." His hand closed over hers and held it tightly. "You'll have good and bad times in your life, and you've got to know what to expect from the man you marry."

She could feel the tears threatening to spill over and she struggled to extricate her hand form his. "I've got to go home now," she said urgently.

"Why? Because you're going to cry? Go ahead, let it out. Mathias and your dad have convinced you there really is a Santa Claus, and I've just poked holes into their arguments. It's only natural that you'd want to cry."

Her vision was blurring quickly. "I don't think I can handle much more right now. . . . Thank you, Michael," she stammered, getting to her feet.

He rose then and came around the table, putting his arms around her shoulders and holding her closely. "You can gild brass, Catherine, but it'll never become gold. Be sure of what you want, and be sure what kind of man your husband really is before you get married."

She nodded against his chest, feeling her tears drip onto the fabric of his shirt. "All right," she mumbled through quivering lips. She wasn't certain why Michael's remarks had upset her so terribly, but they had. Was it because she didn't want to look at marriage in the harsh light he had presented? Or was it because she couldn't admit that she really didn't know Mathias all that well? Slowly she pulled out of his gentle embrace.

His eyes were grave as he studied her. "Okay, go on home. But remember, Catherine, I'm here. If you're ever confused about anything, or if you need a shoulder to cry on, you can always come to me for help. I care a great deal about you, you know, and I want to see you happy."

For some reason, his gentle reassurance made her

want to cry all the more. Turning with a sob, she ran blindly out of the kitchen.

Once back in her own room, she threw herself across her bed and wept for a long, long time. Her heart ached profusely and she yearned to be comforted—but by whom? Her mind floundered in a confusing whirlpool of doubt.

Chapter 12

All that afternoon, Catherine tried to decide what she should do. She felt terribly depressed and not at all able to think clearly. Michael's lecture plagued her and clouded her introspection. Except for the bitter loss of her mother, Catherine's life had always been rather sheltered. She had never wanted for anything, had never gone hungry, and her father's indomitable control over her life had resulted in the fact that she had never really learned to fight for what she wanted. To be sure, she had occasionally had to maneuver her father, like the time she had wanted to leave the Sorbonne and study photography, but that had hardly entailed a genuinely dramatic clash of wills.

Even when she was living in Paris and going to school, her life had been free from strife. Her father had sent her a comfortable allowance, with which she had been expected to take care of her needs. It had meant that she had had to budget her money, but even at that she had been far better off than many of her classmates had been.

In a vague sort of way, Catherine knew that she liked the idea of being Mrs. Mathias Brunton. He seemed to know what he wanted from life and how to get it. He was also a strong person, who believed, as Mr. Moreau did, that the man in the household made the decisions . . . and she secretly rather liked the idea of not having to make major decisions by herself. She found Mathias highly attractive, and she knew that life with him would never be dull. For one thing, so much entertaining would be necessary—for business, if nothing else. Catherine had become accustomed to going out, to being seen in the right places, and she was enjoying herself immensely. What was so wrong, she rationalized, about accepting his proposal in the firm belief that their lives would always be like that?

But the way Michael had spoken, it was as if the rug might be pulled out from under her at any second; as if every day of marriage would be like teetering on the brink of disaster. She didn't want to look at life in that way—why should she? Nothing terrible had ever happened to her security with her father, so why should it with Mathias? Besides, if she married Mathias, she was confident that her father would turn the business over to him when he retired. Then Mathias would be president of Moreau Electronics, which was part of a booming industry. No, she decided, Michael hadn't been looking at her situation clearly . . . or maybe he had been projecting his own fears about matrimony.

There wasn't a reason she could think of as to why she shouldn't expect to have a wonderful life with Mathias. As for her career, well, she could always decide about that later on. Perhaps Mathias was right; maybe the role of being his wife would be entirely too demanding for her to juggle a career, as well. Besides, photography wasn't something a person forgot; she could continue with it as her hobby.

As the afternoon wore on, Catherine began to feel more relaxed and positive about the prospect of marrying Mathias. There was no doubt in her mind that Mathias loved her very much, and that had to count for a great deal in their future together. If she were still a little uncertain about her own feelings, well, perhaps she just didn't know what to expect and that it would all fall into place later. Tingles and butterflies were what novelists wrote about, but Catherine wasn't all that certain they were universal requirements to being in love. Perhaps they would come later, after marriage; or maybe never at all. But could they be more important than having an adoring husband?

By three o'clock, as the July sun started to beat on the west side of the house, Catherine's bedroom became oppressively warm and she decided to go downstairs and make herself a sandwich. As she reached the bottom of the stairs, she noticed Josephine sitting in the living room and reading a book with a magnifying glass. "What juicy scandal are you reading about?" she asked jokingly.

Josephine shook her head as she looked up. "I'm not. I'm reading about France's involvement in Vietnam."

"You're *what*?" Catherine couldn't suppress a shocked laugh. In her twenty-two years, she had never known the woman to read anything but magazines and mystery stories.

She nodded vigorously. "When Michael was here last week I made some remark about the Americans in Vietnam. He scolded me severely, saying I had better know something about our own country's influence before I criticized someone else's."

"I see," Catherine said, still amused. "So he's got you onto that path, as well, has he?"

"And he's right. We should know what we're talking about before we spout our opinions, or else we should keep our mouths shut."

Catherine leaned against the frame of the door, and her slate blue eyes looked at the woman affectionately. "You like Michael, don't you?" she stated.

"Of course. He's an intelligent young man and very dedicated. I think that's admirable in this day and age."

"I sometimes think he's a little too heavy-handed about it. He takes everything so seriously."

"Are we discussing the same Michael? I find him to have an excellent sense of humor, and he's quite fond of a good laugh."

Catherine shook her head. "Oh, yes, he does . . . but I mean about his work." She had been about to add the word "marriage" as well, but decided against it.

"And why not? I've lived through two world wars, Catherine, and the older I get, the more I realize that they could have been averted if people had paid more attention to what was happening around them."

"I give up," Catherine said, smiling. "You're hooked, I can tell."

Josephine's mouth compressed with annoyance. "It wouldn't hurt you, Catherine, if you were to keep up with the news instead of gallivanting till all hours of the night."

Catherine went into the room and sat down near the old governess. "That time may be closer than you think," she said quietly. "I'm thinking of marrying Mathias."

The woman gasped softly, then looked away.

Leaning forward, Catherine asked, "You don't approve?"

"It's not up to me, child," Josephine said in a low voice.

"But you don't like the idea," Catherine pursued.

"Since you're asking, no, I don't."

"Is it because you object to Mathias?"

Josephine put her magnifying glass down and closed her book. "I've never had much occasion to talk with him, Catherine. I don't really know him. Your father is probably a better judge of his character than I am."

"Then what is it?"

Her dark eyes were almost obsidian as they looked at Catherine. "It's you, child. You're entirely too young for marriage . . . oh, not in years, but in your heart and mind. When you defied your father to make a career of your own, I was very happy for you. The world you had chosen for yourself was one where you would meet many interesting people and would have a chance to learn and grow as a person. But now you want to forget about all that and marry the first man who asks you."

"I'll be marrying someone some day, Josephine—why not Mathias? Besides, if I let him go now, I may never have a chance to change my mind. Mathias is thirty-two and he wants to settle down. . . . If I don't marry him, another woman will."

Josephine snorted. "Are we talking about adults or brood mares? What kind of foolishness is in your head? You don't jump into marriage simply because if you don't, someone else will snap up your man. . . . The point is in finding happiness through sharing, Catherine."

"I know that," she said softly.

"I wonder if you do," Josephine said under her breath. "And what about Michael?"

"Michael! What does he have to do with this?"

Josephine shook her head slowly, a pained expression in her eyes. "If you haven't figured that out, then obviously there's no point in mentioning it now. Oh, how I wish your mother . . . ." But Josephine suddenly caught herself. "Have you told Mr. Brunton your decision yet?"

"I'll tell him tonight," Catherine said, wishing herself that she could talk to her mother about it all. "We're going out to dinner at a new restaurant on the Boulevard Montmartre."

"I hope you're doing the right thing, child," she said, her eyes brimming with tears.

THEY WERE SEATED at a corner table near a cozy fireplace and surrounded by plants and vines. The restaurant had been decorated as if it were a greenhouse, which helped considerably to keep the noise level down. Catherine was surprised to see how crowded it was even though it had just opened. She and Mathias had already said hello to some of their friends as they'd entered, and Mathias was in a particularly good mood.

"You must have bagged a big account," Catherine said.

"No, it has nothing to do with the factory. A small, uh, investment I made a few months ago has paid off handsomely."

"Speaking of which," Catherine said, watching the wine steward fill her glass halfway, "I've been meaning to clarify something you said. Remember when I mentioned that father had told me you had a trust fund?"

"Yes. Why?"

"Well, he said that it was from a deceased aunt. But when I mentioned it to you, you said it was an uncle. It's not important, of course, but I was just curious as to which was right."

Mathias's eyes became guarded and almost wary. "I, uh, well, I may have told your father it was an aunt," he said cautiously. "In a way, it was both. My aunt and uncle were, uh, killed in an airplane accident a few years ago. I was living in Tangiers at the time and—"

"Tangiers! But you never told me that," Catherine exclaimed excitedly. "When was that? What were you doing in such an exotic place?"

Mathias exhaled heavily. "It wasn't a very pleasant period in my life, Catherine. I would prefer not to discuss it, if you don't mind."

Catherine had already learned that when Mathias said he preferred something, it was actually an order. She let the subject drop, but it baffled her that he had lived abroad and had never once mentioned the fact. Perhaps he had had love affair in Tangiers that had broken his heart. . . . Why else would Mathias not want to talk about it?

"I'm glad to see you wearing your necklace, Catherine. It looks stunning with that dress—just the right touch."

"Thank you, Mathias," she replied, her small hand touching the baguette of stones. She suddenly recalled Michael telling her that her mother had referred to her cameo as "a gift of love." Would she one day feel the same way about this necklace? She hoped so.

"You seem very wistful and dreamy, darling. Any special reason?"

Her lips tucked into a shy smile. "Yes."

His fingers linked through hers across the table. "And do I get to know why?"

"I've decided," she began, almost bashfully, "to marry you, Mathias."

"What? Can I believe my ears?" His expression was jubilant and incredulous. "Do you mean it?"

"Yes," she answered, pleased to see how happy he was.

"Darling, you've made me the happiest of all men," he said, leaning across the table and kissing her lightly on the lips. "When? When can we set the date?"

"Wait, wait," she protested, laughing. "We have to be engaged first, remember? I thought, Mathias, that it might be nice to have an announcement party. . . . I know father will be pleased and will probably agree. Then, afterward, we should spend some time together alone, so we can get to know each other better."

"I know as much about you now as I need to," Mathias said, a touch of disappointment in his voice.

"But I'm not nearly as complex a personality as you are, Mathias. I really know very little about you, if you think about it . . . that you lived in Tangiers, for instance."

His expression clouded and Catherine instantly took a different tack. "I know nothing about your life as a child, who your parents are or what college you went to. . . . I only know the person I met in March. I'm very fond of you, Mathias, and I think I love you . . . but I don't want to rush into it."

"You're right," he said, cupping her hand and bringing it to his smooth-shaven cheek. "Tomorrow we'll get the engagement ring, and I promise that we'll spend as many quiet evenings together as we can."

"Then I think we can plan the wedding for a year from now . . . or maybe even June, if you wish."

"But that's so far away, Catherine. I don't know if I can stand waiting that long."

"Of course you can," she said innocently, but with youthful confidence. "I'd like to have a large wedding, and we'll need time to plan for it."

Mathias then plunged into their plans for the future. They would honeymoon in Spain, he decided, staying at the magnificent *paradores*, which were really converted castles. They would drive from Barcelona down to Valencia, then over to Andalusia, where they would visit Malaga and Seville. Their wedding would be spectacular, and everyone who was anyone in Paris would be present—and she would be the most beautiful bride in all history!

Throughout dinner, which Catherine in her excitement hardly tasted, Mathias talked ebulliently. They would have three children, each spaced about two years apart. "And, of course, we'll have to start shopping for a house right away. My apartment is fine for a bachelor, but not at all suitable for my bride and our future children. Or perhaps we should get a townhouse right in Paris," he suggested. "Would you like that?"

"It would be awfully far for you to commute to work," she answered practically. "Besides, it would cost a fortune."

"Maybe your father could help us out a little."

"Well," she said, smiling, "we have plenty of time to worry about that. Which is another reason for not getting married at once. It takes time to find the right house, and at a price we'll be able to afford. Then we'd have to furnish it, and that, too, costs money."

"Money, money, money! You're preoccupied with it, my darling. I'm doing very well and I plan to do even better! You mustn't fret about those things, Catherine. That's my department, all right?"

She bobbed her head, wondering why he was so reluctant to discuss such matters but content to let it rest on his shoulders. Mathias continued talking animatedly about their future, and Catherine was becoming more certain that her decision was the right one as each moment passed. He was like a little boy with his first electric train, hardly able to contain his delight. Then, abruptly, he frowned and stared past Catherine. Inexplicably, his expression froze.

"What's wrong?" She started to twist in her chair to see what had interrupted him.

"No, don't turn around. But let's get out of here," he said authoritatively.

"But why? We haven't finished our coffee yet and you haven't paid the bill. . . ."

"We can have coffee somewhere else, and I'll pay the bill on the way out. Don't argue with me, Catherine. A fellow just came in whom I had hoped never to see again—an unfortunate old acquaintance who should be forgotten, as the song goes. I just want to get out of here as quickly as possible!"

She had been about to ask if it was someone he had known in Tangiers, but realized it would be an unwelcome question. He was already upset enough. Whomever he was avoiding, surely he had good reason for it, and he would tell her about it later.

Caught off guard and more than a little surprised, she quickly gathered up her small handbag and the light wrap she had draped over the back of her chair.

Mathias was casual in a studied way as he stood up and held Catherine's chair for her. Not once did he look back toward whomever it was he wanted to avoid— a person, Catherine sensed, whom Mathias feared. . . .

Chapter 13

By the end of the following month Catherine's life had become even more magical than it had been in the previous four. The announcement party on August 11 had been a huge success, and now that the engagement was official, the wives of Mathias's friends were inviting her to teas and including her in their daytime outings.

While she and Mathias did socialize somewhat less frequently in the evenings, she soon realized that his business just couldn't be shut out that easily, and obviously being seen in chic places and entertaining was a very important part of his success. Catherine also came to accept the fact that Mathias loved an active nightlife, and she didn't have the heart to protest too strongly. After all, it was his glittering world that she had found so appealing in the first place. . . . Why should she try to change it or him? She was confident that after they were married their life-style would settle down considerably.

Even Mr. Moreau's attitude had improved toward her. Unfortunately, however, Roberta had been making a nuisance of herself by insisting she help with the wedding plans. Then she volunteered to go house hunting, as well, and kept phoning Catherine about "adorable" places that turned out to be anything but suitable for their purposes. Catherine felt that the woman meant well and was really trying to be helpful, so she couldn't very well take offense.

Being the future Mrs. Mathias Brunton had caused a noticeable difference in the way almost everyone treated her. It was as if she had survived an initiation, or had just been accepted as a citizen. Josephine had taken the news stoically, and if she still didn't approve, she wasn't letting it show. As for Michael, Catherine had hardly seen him in the last five or six weeks. Even though she had invited him to her party, he had thanked her and had given a rather lame excuse—in her opinion—for not attending. In fact, if they hadn't become such good friends, Catherine might have suspected that Michael was avoiding her. But that was too silly to seriously contemplate; why should he?

Her life seemed to have taken a form and purpose she had never before dreamed of. Naturally when she had been in school she had fantasized about becoming a highly successful photographer. There had been periods of doubt, as well, of course, knowing how terribly competitive the field was. But now Catherine had no more worries about direction or purpose; obviously marriage was the epitome of respectability.

Then, on the last Friday of the month, everything changed. She had spent the morning with Louise Morgan, whose husband, Harry, allowed Mathias to ride his horse Windfire. Though the Morgans were considerably older, Catherine had taken a strong liking to Louise, who had a very optimistic outlook on life and a wonderfully whimsical sense of humor.

Catherine got back to St. Cloud around eleven-thirty and was surprised to see Josephine standing at the living-room window as if waiting for her. "Hi," she called as she entered the foyer.

"Thank God you're home!" Josephine exclaimed, her eyes obviously reddened from crying.

"What's wrong?" Catherine had never seen the woman so distraught, and she knew something terrible must have happened.

"It's . . . it's . . . ." Josephine broke into tears again.

Feeling her fears mounting by the second, Catherine gently put her arms around her former governess. "Shh, Josephine, it can't be that bad. Please, won't you tell me what's happened?"

"It's . . . your f-father," Josephine blurted at last. "He's had a heart attack . . . they took him to the h-hospital about an hour ago."

"Father!" Catherine's mind reeled with the news. He'd always been in perfect health! "Which hospital, Josephine?"

"Th-the Du Val de Grace . . . his s-secretary, Mrs. Simpson, telephoned t-to let y-you know," she stammered, still choking with sobs.

"Have you called to find out what's happening? Is he in intensive care or . . .?"

Josephine shook her head, tears streaming down her lined cheeks. "They w-won't tell me anything, Catherine! Th-they said I have to b-be his wife or a relative!"

"But that's ridiculous!" Catherine said, half furious with the hospital policy and half terrified that her father might have already died. "I'll call right now," she said firmly.

"I've known him since he was just a little boy, hardly able to walk," Josephine babbled to herself.

Catherine strode to the telephone in her father's office and looked up the number for the hospital. She asked for the emergency room, figuring that that was probably where they would have taken him first. When the receptionist answered, she said, "I'm calling about my father, Pierre Moreau, who was admitted a short while ago with a heart attack."

There was a brief silence, then the nurse came back on. "Yes, he was admitted into E.R. thirty-five minutes ago, but he's been transferred."

"What's his room number?"

"I don't know, miss, you'll have to ask Admissions."

"Can you connect me to them?"

"Yes, miss. . . ."

"Wait! Before you do, how is he?"

"Beg your pardon, miss?"

"I asked how he is," she repeated, her impatience obvious in her voice.

"I really couldn't say, miss. You'll have to ask the doctor about his condition."

The woman was being so impersonal that Catherine wished she could shake her. "Is the doctor there?"

"No, he's not."

"Then how do you expect me to ask him anything?"

"Look, miss, this is an emergency room, not a secretarial service. We're not permitted to discuss the patients . . . right now."

"Can you at least tell me where they've taken him? Is he in intensive care? Is he still alive?"

"I'll connect you to Admissions," the nurse said efficiently, and put Catherine on hold before she could protest.

"What does she say?" Josephine asked, standing next to Catherine with a heartbroken expression in her eyes.

"He's been moved, but that's all I know right—" Catherine held up her hand as another voice came on.

"Admissions," a woman said.

Again Catherine went through the litany and asked to be connected to her father's room. Her hands had become clammy with tension and fear.

"Moreau," the woman said, then verified the spelling. "Yes, he's in Room 211, but he's not permitted any calls."

"May I speak to the floor nurse, then?"

"One moment, please."

Catherine tried to smile encouragingly at Josephine, but the pained expression in the woman's eyes told her it was useless. The floor nurse came on the line just as Catherine glanced at her watch. She'd been trying to find out how her father was for nearly five minutes! "I'm Pierre Moreau's daughter," she began. "I believe he's in Room 211, is that correct?"

"Yes, ma'am. But he's not to be disturbed."

"I know that," Catherine said impatiently, then tried to calm down. "Is there a Mr. Brunton there in the waiting room?"

"There was a young man in here a little while ago, but the doctor sent him home. I don't know his name, miss. I'm sorry."

"Would it be possible to speak to the doctor, then?"

"I'll have him paged, if you like."

"Yes, yes! Thank you, nurse. In the meantime, can you tell me how my father is?"

"Well," the woman said cautiously "I think it's all right to tell you his condition has stabilized."

Heaving a sigh of relief, Catherine reached out and took Josephine's bony hand, nodding that it wasn't as bad as she had feared. "Thank you, nurse . . . I genuinely appreciate your kindness."

"I'll page Dr. Petri for you, miss."

Josephine sank into a chair and covered her face, but at least this time Catherine knew it was from gratitude instead of from fear. After a few more minutes, the physician came on the line and explained that her father was doing as well as could be expected, and that if his condition remained the same overnight, she could visit him in the morning, but only for a little while.

"Will he be all right, doctor?" Though he had already assured her that her father wasn't in any immediate danger, she had to hear it again.

"It's rather soon to predict that, Miss Moreau. It looks pretty good right now. However, a lot will depend on what happens over the next twelve hours. If he should happen to have another attack on the heels of this one, well, that would change the prognosis considerably. But we have him sedated, and there's no point worrying about things we can't predict. The main thing is not to upset him. If you visit him tomorrow, try to appear as natural and relaxed as possible."

Catherine could hear the physician being paged in the background and she knew he had to get off the telephone. "All right, Dr. Petri. Thank you. I'll phone back in the morning." She replaced the receiver and went to comfort Josephine. "We might be able to see him in the morning," she said soothingly.

"They won't let me, child," she said, regaining control of herself. "I'm not a relative."

Catherine smiled down at her. "Why, Josephine,

how could you forget that Pierre Moreau is your son?
I'm shocked!''

"Do you think they'd believe us?'' the old woman
asked hopefully.

"How would they know the difference?'' Catherine
replied with as much playfulness as she could muster.
For the moment, she knew there was nothing she could
do for her father. But Josephine was well into her sev-
enties, and Catherine wasn't happy about the pallor
of her complexion after the shock of the news. Her
primary concern right then was to try to lessen Josephine's worries, and she felt that a little levity might
help the situation.

AROUND ONE O'CLOCK Mathias called her from the factory. He sounded rather tired, which Catherine assumed was directly connected with her father's attack.
"Were you with him when it happened?'' she asked.

"Practically speaking,'' Mathias answered. "I could
hear him bawling out the production manager even
from my office, so I was heading down to find out
what the problem was when he had the attack. In the
six years I've worked with Pierre, I've never heard him
really raise his voice, so I knew it must be pretty serious.''

"I can't even imagine him shouting at anyone,'' she
said truthfully. "You did go with him to the hospital,
didn't you?''

"They wouldn't let me into the ambulance, so I took
my own car. Once they had taken him up to his own
room and I had spoken with the doctor, I came straight
back here.''

"Then what took you so long to telephone me?'' she

inquired. "You must have been back at least an hour ago."

"Be reasonable, darling—there were a lot of very upset employees around here, and a lot of questions to be answered. That's why I had Mrs. Simpson telephone your house at once; I knew I'd be tied up for a while and that you'd have the sense to call the hospital on your own."

"Poor Mrs. Simpson," Catherine said. "How did she take it?"

Mathias gave a half laugh. "I sent her home when I got back—she was a nervous wreck. But this is a big factory, darling, and the employees had to be reassured that their jobs weren't in jeopardy. You have to remember that your father is the sole head of this company, and there's no second-in-command. Naturally they feared that if anything happened to him the place would shut down."

"Hasn't he set up any chain of authority for emergencies?"

"None that any of us knows about," Mathias said.

They spoke a little longer, and Mathias promised to come to St. Cloud the moment he could get away from the plant. He explained that he would have to make an early evening of it so that he could assume the responsibilities of Moreau Electronics while her father was gone, but that later on he'd tell her in more detail what had happened.

When she got off the phone, she found Josephine in the kitchen, staring out the window as if she were in another world. "Why don't you lie down, Josephine?" she suggested. "You look worn out."

The housekeeper turned and gazed affectionately at

Catherine. "You're probably right, child. Did Mr. Brunton say what caused your father's attack?"

Catherine shrugged. "Only briefly . . . something about the production manager telling him that the plant would strike if the workers didn't get a raise in pay."

"There has to be more to it than that," the woman said.

"Well, maybe he can tell us more when he gets here. Please go rest, Josephine."

"What about you, child?"

Catherine smiled. "I think Michael is home. I want to go next door and see if he can take us to the hospital in the morning. For that matter, he doesn't even know what's happened yet. I'll be back in a little while, but I'll take the phone off the hook so you won't be disturbed."

She watched Josephine leave the room with a slow, shuffling movement and realized that the woman must be exhausted from the emotional strain she had been through. Glancing around the kitchen, she was almost sorry that she had told Mrs. Campbell not to come in that day. Catherine had already fixed soup and sandwiches for herself and Josephine, but now she would also have to think of what to prepare for dinner. Opening the freezer side of the refrigerator, she inspected the contents. Finally she spotted a roast of beef and took it out; it would be easy to prepare and would save her the task of trying to think of something more imaginative to serve to Mathias. This was going to be the first time he would ever taste her cooking—which, admittedly, wasn't her strong point—and she didn't want to disappoint him too badly.

Putting the meat on the sideboard to thaw, Catherine

took the phone off the hook and quietly let herself out of the house. Scant seconds later she was standing at the French windows to Michael's dining room, where she rapped firmly.

He didn't appear right away, and she had just begun to turn away when the door opened behind her. "Hello, Catherine. What a nice surprise," Michael said.

Suddenly, as if all the events of the morning had come crashing down around her, Catherine threw herself into his arms and clung tightly.

"Whoa, there—what is it?"

She smiled feebly against his strong chest, then pulled away. "I've been brave for about as long as I can take it," she said, laughing at herself. "I just needed someone to hold me up, I guess." She then proceeded to tell him about her father's heart attack.

"Well," he said, tousling her hair lightly, "I can appreciate your needing a strong arm to lean on for a few moments." By this time they had gone into the living room and Michael had insisted she have a brandy to brace herself. "Now, what can I do to help?"

Catherine smiled thankfully at him. "I knew I could count on you, Michael. You really are the best friend I have."

"I'm glad you know that," he replied quietly, his dark brown eyes enveloping her warmly.

"Would you take Josephine and me to the hospital tomorrow if the doctor says it's all right?"

"Sure. What time?"

"About nine in the morning?"

Michael pulled out his small appointment book and glanced at it briefly. "I have an appointment with the Minister of Commerce at eight-thirty, but I'll change it."

"Oh, no! You mustn't cancel your plans, Michael! We can always take the bus or the subway. . . . I don't want to interfere with your career."

He grinned. "It's not interfering, Catherine. I want to do it—in fact, I insist." He got up and crossed the room to a small writing desk, which had a telephone on it. "An offer to help should never be accompanied with a lot of conditions and strings. Besides, I don't think Josephine could manage public transportation anymore."

When the party he had dialed answered the phone, she heard him asking to speak with the minister's secretary. As Michael arranged to change the time of his appointment, Catherine couldn't help thinking what a wonderful person he was and how lucky she was to know someone who was so willing to go out of his way to help her.

"There, that's taken care of. At your disposal, Miss Moreau—the doctors willing."

Filled with gratitude she stood up and started moving toward the door. "Why don't you come over and have dinner with us tonight?" she asked spontaneously. "It'll just be Josephine, you and me, and of course, Mathias."

Michael frowned slightly and his eyes became veiled. "I've got some work to do tonight, Catherine. But thanks anyhow. Besides, I think you and your fiancé should have the chance to discuss what you're going to do while your father's incapacitated."

"Do? What do you mean?"

"It won't be the same, Catherine. There will have to be some changes made in your life, and that should just be between you and Mathias."

He ushered her to the door and waved her off, saying

he'd see her in the morning. Yet there was something about his manner that had made Catherine a little tense. What changes could he possibly have meant? Her father would convalesce and then things would return to normal . . . wouldn't they?

Chapter 14

Mr. Moreau was discharged on Monday with instructions to stay in bed and get plenty of rest for the next week; and of course, going to the factory was out of the question. He was supposed to take it easy, and return to his normal life only gradually, while including a regimen of moderate exercise in his schedule every day. The fact that he had kept himself in trim condition, fortunately, had worked in his favor. But he was going to have to stop smoking cigars and drinking any form of alcohol for at least three months till the doctors saw how he was recuperating.

Mathias took the morning off from work to bring Mr. Moreau home in his own car, and Josephine hovered over him as if he were still a little boy.

"Easy, now," Mathias said, as he helped the older man get out of the passenger side of the car.

"Josephine, open the front door, please," Catherine said as she put her arm around her father's waist so he could lean on her. It seemed to take forever for him to walk up to the steps, and it almost broke Catherine's heart to see how he had to labor to climb them.

Finally they had him inside and seated in his favorite

chair in the living room. His breathing was uneven and his face had become quite flushed. "I'll be all right in a moment," he said with difficulty. "The doctor told me to expect this difficulty for the first week or so."

"Don't bother to talk, father," Catherine said, putting a blanket around his legs. It was a dull, overcast day and despite the time of year there was a chill in the air. As she straightened up and looked at him, all the feelings of resentment she had ever had toward him vanished. Whatever she had experienced in the past had no bearing on the fact that he needed her now, and in a way, Catherine was glad. She loved her father and always had, but she had had to develop a shell to protect herself from his lack of warmth and demonstrativeness. Maybe now all that would change, she thought. Perhaps, for the first time in her life, she might get to know him as a person, to understand him. . . . In time they might even become friends.

"Is his room ready?" Mathias asked, seating himself on the couch.

"Yes. Josephine and I brought everything downstairs to the guest room," Catherine replied. "Once he's rested a bit, you can help us move him in there and get him into bed."

"Of course," he said.

"Roberta's coming over this afternoon, so she'll keep him company for a while. Knowing father as I do, I think boredom is going to be his biggest enemy."

Still a bit flushed, but breathing more regularly, Mr. Moreau nodded. "I've never been sick a day in my life," he said slowly.

"Well," Josephine said, "there are books and magazines and television. I'll be here, and so will Catherine. . . ."

"And I'll come over every evening after work so you'll know how things are going at the plant."

"Does that damn fool still think he's going to call a strike?" Mr. Moreau asked, his face getting red again.

"Now, let's not talk about that right now," Josephine said sternly.

"She's right, Pierre. We can discuss that later, when you're feeling better. But for now, everyone has agreed to leave things as they are. You don't have a thing to worry about," Mathias affirmed.

Josephine excused herself, offering to make a pot of tea for them all, as well as a cup of broth for the patient, who wasn't supposed to have any kind of stimulants.

Gradually Mr. Moreau's color returned to normal and he seemed glad just to be home again. "While I've got you both together," he said after a while, "I want to ask something of you."

"Certainly, father. What is it?"

"It won't be too difficult," he began, his gray eyes moving quickly from Catherine to Mathias. "I want you two to get married right away."

Mathias looked at Catherine inquiringly. "For me, it would be a blessing."

"But father, we weren't planning the wedding until spring or early next summer. Why should we change that?" Catherine was trying to remain calm, but inside she was churning. She had counted on a long engagement to make certain of her feelings toward Mathias, yet she didn't want to upset her father by refusing his request.

Mr. Moreau stared hard at her for a few moments, then, as if pained, he glanced away. "I want my world in order, Catherine. It never occurred to me that I might become ill or die suddenly—but my heart attack has changed that. I had a lot of time to think while I was in the hospital. I now see that if I were to die unexpectedly, many people's lives would be turned upside down needlessly." He paused to catch his breath. "I've telephoned both my personal and corporate attorneys, and they'll come by later in the week to set things up properly."

"I think that's a sound move, Pierre." Mathias broke in. "There was near panic last Friday after the ambulance took you off. No one knew what to do or who to listen to, so of course I took charge when I got back to the office. With your permission, I'd be happy to continue in that role till you come back."

For a split second, Catherine was irked by Mathias's tone and attitude. There was something almost smooth in his manner as if he expected a bonus or some other form of recompense for what he had done. But then Catherine realized that she was being unfair. After all, Mathias had assumed the responsibility on his own, and he had no way of knowing if her father approved of his action.

"Yes, Mathias, that would be fine. However, I want you to start learning more about the production end of the business. I want you to know every step involved so I can rely on you to handle any problem that comes up, big or small."

"Of course, Pierre. It won't take me long."

"No, I know it won't. It would make me feel much better if I knew I had someone in the company who could stand in for me. Obviously, I shall now have to spend less time at the factory than I used to."

"But father," Catherine said, "Dr. Petri made it perfectly clear that once you've recovered, you'll be able to do almost anything you want to do. As he said this morning, a minor heart attack is often a blessing. It's nature's way of warning us not to overwork, but that's not the same thing as retiring."

"Be that as it may, Catherine, I have had to face my own mortality. There are no guarantees, and having had one attack, I may have another—and the next one might not be so minor."

"Of course, father," she said, amazed at the change in him.

"There are some very important things that I must attend to in the next few weeks, but I'll rest more comfortably if I know everything is in order."

"It will be, Pierre, I'm sure," Mathias said.

"Which is why I want you two to get married right away," Mr. Moreau continued, looking at Mathias. "I want to be sure that Catherine's future is secure. I don't know if I'll even be alive next year. This wedding should take place before the end of September, Mathias. Agreed?"

Mathias smiled in agreement as Catherine's mind grappled with this sudden change. "But father," she said quickly, "that's too soon! My gown has to be ordered and invitations sent. And where will we live? I don't think you should be talking about dying like this . . . it's not a healthy attitude!"

The older man shook his head slowly. "There are such things as rush orders, you know. People can accomplish wonderful feats when they're paid overtime," he argued. "You can live in Mathias's apartment. Or if that's too small, you could even live here. There's plenty of room. I won't be going upstairs anymore, Catherine. You could redecorate the master bedroom and stay until you find a home of your own."

"Father! I won't have you talking like that! You're

making an invalid of yourself and it's not at all necessary!"

"Why are you taking that tone of voice with your father?" Josephine asked as she came back into the room carrying a tray.

Mathias got to his feet and took it from her, then set it on the low table in front of the sofa. He looked at Catherine, his blue green eyes fixed on hers. "I know you want more time, darling, but let's not upset your father with some minor protests. I love you, Catherine, and you'll just have to trust that I shall always take care of you. There's no real reason why we can't get married right away—only your fears about not knowing me long enough."

"Well, *I've* known you long enough," Mr. Moreau said, "and I can vouch for your character, Mathias." He folded his hands in his lap and gazed down at them. "I would consider it a great favor, Catherine, if you would consent."

She gazed at her father, sympathy washing through her. He seemed so helpless, so totally unlike the forceful man she had known all her life. Had the doctor given him a different verdict from the one he'd given her? Did her father possess more information than he was letting on? He seemed so adamant about his condition, as if he was certain that he had very little time left. . . . Could she deny him this one request? After all, she had loved Mathias enough to become engaged to him . . . would another few months of waiting really make a difference?

"All right, father," Catherine said meekly. "We'll plan it for the last Saturday in September. I don't know how we'll manage, but we shall . . . if it makes you happy."

"It will, Catherine, it will."

"This is wonderful!" Mathias said, kissing Catherine's cheek.

Josephine was pouring the tea, and as she handed some to Catherine, her hand was shaking so much that the cup rattled in the suacer.

BY THE WEEK before the wedding, most of the guests had replied to their invitations. Catherine had gone into Paris for the final fitting of her wedding dress. The couturiere was one that Roberta had recommended and was located on the fashionable Champs Élysées.

It had been a strenuous period for Catherine, trying to get too much done in too little time. Fortunately, being so busy had prevented her from having second thoughts about her decision to marry Mathias. If anything, she had become caught up in the excitement of the preparations. Moreover, Mathias had been wonderful throughout it all. Of course, the fact that Mr. Moreau had appointed Mathias as vice-president of Moreau Electronics had only augmented his optimism.

As Catherine was leaving the couturiere's establishment, she thought she recognized a tall young man coming out of the Air France office, and she rushed to catch up with him. "Michael! It *is* you!"

He turned and looked down at her, a pleased and surprised expression in his dark brown eyes. "Catherine! This is wonderful! What brings you to this part of town?"

"Or what brings you, for that matter?"

"I was just getting a refund. I had planned to begin my vacation next week, but something else has come up so I've canceled my reservation. Say, how about having a bite of lunch with me? There's a nice little café just a couple of blocks away."

She glanced at her watch. "I'll have to telephone Josephine so she doesn't worry about me."

"That's all right," he said, taking her by the elbow. "There isn't a shortage of pay phones in this city."

Feeling suddenly daring, as if she were playing hooky, Catherine smiled broadly. "Okay, let's go."

On the way to the restaurant, Michael inquired about her father and seemed genuinely distressed to learn how he seemed to be reacting to the attack. Once they were seated at a table, Michael frowned. "Doesn't he know that thousands of people have heart attacks all the time and go on to live full and productive lives?"

"That's what I keep telling him, Michael, but he doesn't seem to believe me. I even called Dr. Petri and insisted he give me the full truth about father's condition."

"What did he say?"

She shrugged. "That there's not a reason in the world to worry about him as long as he doesn't work himself to death. I told Dr. Petri that father still hasn't gone back to work, that he just lolls listlessly around the house, and the doctor said that it was just foolish and pointless self-pampering."

"Would the doctor be willing to speak to your father?" Michael wanted to know. "Maybe he'd listen to reason if it came from a physician."

"Dr. Petri offered to, but if he has actually done so, father hasn't mentioned it. As it is, I think there's something else on father's mind. He seems to be watching me all the time, and he won't let anyone in the house answer the phone. He's made it a strict rule— either he answers the phone or we let it ring."

"That's strange," Michael said, perplexed.

"It certainly is!" Catherine concurred. "Even Roberta, who dotes on him hand and foot, thinks he's carrying it too far. I don't know what to make of his behavior, but I don't dare upset him. I'd never forgive myself if he had another attack because of something I said or did."

"Yes, I can understand that. But don't you have any idea of what's got into him?"

"Other than his attack, no."

"Well, I *have* heard of people developing a sort of paranoia following a serious illness. Maybe that's what's happened to your dad."

"What do you mean?"

Michael smiled ruefully. "Oh, a patient might get a feeling that people are talking about him, or even conspiring against him. It's the point about not letting anyone else but himself answer the phone that sounds like he might be going through that."

"Well, he hasn't been listening at keyholes or bursting into rooms unannounced. No, Michael, I think his behavior is connected to his heart attack somehow. He seems so convinced that he'll never be all right again . . . that he may die soon."

"If he keeps thinking that way," Michael said, "sooner or later he'll bring it on himself."

"That's what I'm afraid of," Catherine replied. "And, of course, that was one of my main reasons—if not the only reason—why I agreed to change the wedding date. By the way, you haven't sent me your R.S.V.P. yet. Will you be coming to the reception?"

Michael leaned back in his chair and crossed his arms. There was a distant look in his eyes. then, taking a deep breath, he rubbed the side of his lean, angular face. "I don't think so, Catherine."

"But why not? Really, Michael! You didn't come to my engagement party last month, and now you won't come to the reception. You and I have become such close friends, and you've been so kind and helpful. . . . Why won't you come?"

He laughed incredulously. "You really don't know, do you?" he commented flatly.

"Know what? It'll probably be the most important occasion in my entire life," she pleaded earnestly, "and I want you to share it with me!"

He bowed his head for a second, then gazed into her eyes thoughtfully. "Please don't get me wrong, Catherine, but I think you're making a terrible mistake by marrying Mathias."

"Mistake! Why would you say that?"

"I can't give you all the particulars, because I don't have any tangible proof yet. But I've been looking into his background, and I don't like what I've been finding out."

"Into *his* background? How dare you, Michael! Just because you're a reporter doesn't mean you have the right to snoop around in other people's lives!"

Michael nodded his head slightly, as if he'd been expecting this reaction from her. "I have every right, Catherine—as long as it's public information, a matter being of being on record somewhere. You mean a great deal to me and I don't want to see you married to the wrong man and miserable."

"You were supposed to be finding out about mother, not my fiancé! I think what you've done is absolutely despicable!" Catherine was so furious she could hardly speak.

"I *have* found out what I can about your mother, but you've been so busy I haven't had a chance to talk to you about it."

"I think this discussion is just about over, Michael!" She snatched the napkin from her lap and crushed it in her hand, feeling the color rise in her face.

"Don't you want to hear what I learned about your future husband?" His voice was low and serious.

She got to her feet and looked down at him with contempt. "You yourself said you had no proof, Michael, so why should I listen to your allegations? Mathias is supportive and attentive, and he loves me very much."

"Yes, I believe he probably does. But he's not the man you should marry."

"Do you have any other suggestions?" she asked icily.

"Yes," he replied. "Me. I'm in love with you, Catherine."

She was still so angry that her mind hardly registered the meaning of what he had said. "Then I have to assume that you sank to such a . . . such a low . . . level of behavior because you're jealous! And that's even worse, Michael! It's petty and deceitful. I never want to see you again, do you understand? Never!" She grabbed her handbag and turned away before he could say another word.

Outside on the sidewalk, Catherine gritted her teeth with indignation. *And to think I once trusted him*, she fumed to herself. She strode down the street, unmindful of the passersby who turned in surprise at the sight of the beautiful woman with such an intense expression on her face. Her mind was blank from shock—blank except for the word "Never" echoing over and over.

Chapter 15

Catherine stared out the window as the limousine drove smoothly through the suburbs and out into the open country. Her fingers, so carefully manicured for what should have been the happiest day of her life, were twisted together in the folds of her gown, and the fragile lace of her wedding veil framed her frightened face. The man in the dark blue sweater still sat with his back against the door so that he could watch her as well as the road. He didn't try to talk to her again, however.

They drove through Creteil and then past Vaux-le-Vicomte and Melun, and Catherine wondered if they were taking her to Fontainebleau. But as they approached the forest they kept on going, staying on main roads most of the time. The driver occasionally glanced at her in the rearview mirror, but Catherine didn't fear him as much as the thin-faced man in the blue sweater.

She had leaned forward impulsively a couple of times, wanting to ask exactly what it was they wanted with her. But each time the man had glowered at her from beneath his shaggy eyebrows, shaking his head and making no effort to slide open the glass partition. Catherine had no doubt that the man was armed and that he wouldn't have any inhibitions about harming her if she failed to do as he wished. She felt so completely at the mercy of her captors, so totally helpless and frustrated. . . . Perhaps more importantly, she dreaded to think what might have happened to her father when he discovered she was missing. Thank God Josephine was with him, she thought. The old woman would have the sense to telephone for an ambulance at the first hint of another attack.

Several times during the hour and a half that they had been on the road, tears had slid silently down Catherine's cheeks, leaving dark, wet stains on her beautiful wedding gown. She didn't care. All she could feel was a cold, churning confusion. At one moment she would be terrified for her life, and the next she would be reassuring herself that her father would probably pay whatever ranson they wanted. *Poor Mathias*, she thought. *He must be beside himself with worry!* She couldn't bring herself to think about the guests waiting at the church, or those who would arrive later for a reception that wasn't going to take place.

Soon the road signs indicated that they were nearing Montereau, and the huge car turned off onto a side road. She leaned her forehead against the window on her right and stared out at the pastoral beauty with a heavy heart. Mathias would find her, wouldn't he? He would bring whatever money these men wanted and then he would take her home again. Knowing that she was the daughter of such an important man as Pierre Moreau . . . they wouldn't dare hurt her, would they, she wondered. No, no! Of course not. If they telephoned her father right away, it was possible she might even be free before the day was over!

But then she remembered it was Saturday. Mr. Moreau would never be able to get his hands on a large sum of money until Monday when the banks were open. Fresh tears began to brim in her eyes as the realization sank in. She would have to stay with these two thugs overnight! Shaking her head, she prayed that all they wanted was money. She would not permit herself to think of anything else.

After a while they passed through the town of Bray, and almost at once the car turned left onto a gravel road, the entrance of which was flanked by two large stone pillars supporting an open iron gate. The limousine drove slowly along the private road, and as soon as they rounded a curve, a large château came into view. Moments later they had pulled up in front of the broad staircase leading up to the front door of the enormous mansion.

The man in the blue sweater got out of the car and opened the door to the backseat. "Get out," he commanded in a harsh voice.

Much as she hated herself for showing any weakness, Catherine couldn't help weeping as she gathered up the folds of her wedding gown and got out of the car. "W-where have y-you b-brought me . . . w-what do y-you want?" she stammered.

"The boss will see you soon, and then you'll know."

By then the driver had joined them, and he took her firmly by the wrist. "Come this way!" he commanded.

Intimidated and terrified, Catherine hunched her shoulders as if to ward off their blows. "I-I'll come. You don't have to drag me."

Although her knees felt like rubber, she lifted her

skirt and began to climb the stairs. Soon they were inside what looked like a veritable palace, and Catherine's fears were intensified. No one who could afford such a place would possibly want money! Then . . . what did they want?

"Okay, in here," the man in the blue sweater said, opening a carved wooden door.

Catherine entered an elegant salon, whirling around when she heard the heavy door shut behind her and a key turn in the lock. "Oh, my God," she whispered, "please don't let them harm me!"

She stood in the vast room, hardly noticing the treasures it contained. She didn't know if she should sit down, cower in a corner, or try to escape. At the final thought, she gingerly made her way to the windows and looked down. It was a very long drop to the ground, and she realized she wouldn't be able to jump out without breaking a leg or even her neck. And she was hardly dressed for trying to inch her way around the four-inch-wide ledge to find a more suitable way to the ground. No, she would have to stay where she was and wait.

A delicate porcelain clock on an intricately inlaid table chimed and she gave a start. It was one-thirty. By now, Mathias and her father must have already been in touch with the police. It was nearly two hours since she had been abducted.

The sound of the key turning in the lock again caught Catherine's attention, and half in terror, she turned to face the door. It opened slowly, almost as if whoever was standing on the other side of it was equally afraid of seeing her.

After what seemed like an eternity, a man walked into the salon. "Hello, Catherine," he said.

"You! I . . . I . . . ." But words failed her. She was completely stunned, unable to believe the reality of what she was seeing. Her first instinct was to hurl herself at him, kicking and scratching, but something held her back. Fury and relief flooded her being, and both were expressed in her astonished gasp. "Michael!"

His expression was apologetic. "I want you to know that I didn't arrange for this kidnapping—although I admit, I did help a little."

She stared at him incredulously. You mean it was you who put me through this ordeal? You're even more despicable than I thought!"

"Michael's not to blame. . . . I would have done it with or without his help."

Catherine stared as a stunningly dressed woman came into the room. The woman's curly brown hair was done in a stylish fashion, and her trim figure belied the tiny lines about her slate blue eyes. Catherine felt the blood rushing to her head and she thought she was going to faint. She had never—not in any of her wildest dreams—expected this to be happening, and she stood rooted to the floor in shock.

"Yes, Catherine," Michael said quietly, "this is your mother."

The room began to dim and whirl around her as Michael rushed to her side and helped her to a chair. She sank into it automatically, never for a moment tearing her eyes away from the woman before her.

"My poor darling," Edith Moreau said, coming toward her. She bent and kissed the top of Catherine's head. "I'm sorry it had to be done this way, but we had no choice. Your father wouldn't leave the house. He never left you alone for even a moment, so there was no way I could prevent your marriage except by these radical means. I'm so sorry if we frightened you."

Catherine was fascinated in a surreal kind of way, unable to quite grasp what was happening. The woman whom she had believed dead, the mother she had always longed for, was alive and standing in front of her like a mirrored reflection of herself! "Why did he tell me you were dead?" she finally managed to whisper.

Edith smiled wanly. "Because he's an unimaginative fool, darling. It was easier for him to lie than to tell the truth and listen to arguments, that's all. By saying I was dead, he knew you wouldn't seek me out and that you wouldn't ask any questions about our separation." She looked at her daughter carefully, then turned to Michael. "I think she could use a brandy, Michael. Perhaps we all could."

Michael walked to a liquor cabinet in the far corner of the room as Edith Moreau sat down next to her daughter and took her hand. "I've always been with you, Catherine . . . though you never knew it."

"But how?" The warmth of her mother's hand was like a balm, reassuring Catherine that she wasn't hallucinating. What was happening was all too real.

Mrs. Moreau smiled. "Through Josephine."

"She's known all this while that you're alive?"

The woman nodded slowly, a look of deep compassion in her eyes. "She had sworn allegiance to your father, Catherine, by promising never to tell you that I was still alive. I couldn't ask her to betray him . . . it would have killed her. At first she believed his version of what had happened, that I had been unfaithful to him. But later, when I started writing to her to ask about you, I was able to convince her of the truth.

Whatever happened eleven years ago . . . well, I was certainly never untrue to him. I adored him, and," she stood up, gesturing helplessly, "I suppose I still do. He's a pigheaded, pompous, stubborn mule, and he has caused us all needless pain. But I've never been unfaithful."

The woman accepted the glass of cognac that Michael handed her, a pensive look in her eyes. "Over the years, needless to say, I've had time to think a lot about wh. ɬ supposedly happened back then. I've realized how ʊ.azily both Pierre and I acted, but when you're in love like we were, it's hard to act rationally when you've been hurt.

"I'd always. known that there was something between Roberta and Pierre, but I trusted our love enough not to be jealous when she flirted with him. I had felt that the attraction was more on Roberta's part than on his anyway, and I firmly believe that our marriage would last forever. There was no question about it in my mind, and no hint that he doubted it, either.

"The one day, out of the blue, Roberta came to see me. She said she hated to tell me about it, but that she was so shocked and upset about something that she felt it was her duty to do so. Pierre, she said, had made a pass at her and had even tried to get her into bed with him. He had confessed that he loved her, but until then had repressed it for fear of hurting me as well as you.

"I couldn't believe it, but when I tried to reach your father at the office—I had been away for the weekend and had arrived home after he'd left for work—he refused to speak to me. When he came home that night, it was only to throw a few clothes into a suitcase and leave again, and all he would tell me was that he never wanted to see me again.

"Well, it shattered me, realizing that he must actually be in love with Roberta as she had said. I fell to pieces, and all I could think of doing was getting away from him. I went to my brother in Morocco. He and his wife took care of me during my breakdown, which was quite severe.

"When I began to pull out of it at last and find some interest in living again, I got in touch with Josephine. Of course, I had been missing you very badly, but at least I knew that you were happy with your friends in school. Josephine wrote me that Pierre had already told you I was dead. I have no idea what he would have done if I had shown up to disprove his statement. Anyway, at that point, knowing how close you were to Josephine and how secure you were at school, I decided that it would be better to leave things as they were rather than upset and shock you once again. I didn't want you to become a pawn, Catherine, torn between two bickering parents. You had already grown through the stage where you needed me most, and I trusted Josephine to substitute as a mother in my absence. It wasn't easy. I missed you terribly, but I didn't want to harm you even more than you had already been harmed.

"So I stayed on in Tangiers, eventually getting a job and establishing a new life. After a while I even got over my jealousy and forgave your father for breaking my heart and disrupting our happy life as he had. I expected that eventually he would get in touch with me through our lawyers, asking for a divorce so that he could marry Roberta. But he never did. I'm sure it must have been his guilt that kept him from doing so. For eleven years he has maintained a wall of silence—and, according to Josephine, he's lived a solitary life."

Catherine remained speechless for several moments after her mother stopped talking. Finally, in a voice that betrayed how stunned she felt, she managed to say, "I've always felt that Roberta was after father, but not that he was after her."

"With all these years to think about it, I've become certain that she poisoned his mind against me somehow, as well as mine against him," Edith replied. "And I'm sure that's why she married Pierre's brother, Phillip, so that she could be near Pierre at all times."

"I've always sensed that she wanted to marry father."

Edith laughed. "It would be quite a trick . . . as I'm still married to him. Your father has his faults, I agree, but so far he's not a bigamist."

Catherine suddenly turned toward Michael. "Why didn't you tell me that she was alive?" she demanded of him accusingly.

"When could I have? It's been impossible to see you, Catherine, and I didn't want to break the news to you on the telephone. That's why I was so glad to see you last week. I was just about to tell you in the restaurant when you walked out on me."

"How did you find out?" Catherine asked grudgingly.

Michael sat down on a pale green chair near them. "By trying to find out where Edith was buried. When there didn't seem to be any record of it, nor any death notices in the newspapers, I started to become suspicious. I went to the coroner's offices and checked the records there, and again there was nothing about the demise of one Edith Moreau. If your mother had really died, there would have had to have been a record, unless she had died out of the Paris jurisdiction. Putting two and two together, I figured that she might still be alive, and if that were the case, she would have had to pay income taxes. Even if she were living in a foreign country, she would probably file here, as well. I have a buddy who works for the government in the tax division, and through him I located your mother."

"Which, of course, is quite illegal," Mrs. Moreau said, smiling nonetheless. "So much for confidentiality."

"But what about father?" Catherine wanted to know. "He may have another heart attack over this . . . this kidnapping! *He* doesn't know that it is a hoax."

"But it isn't a hoax, Catherine. It's very real, and the only difference is we're not asking for money."

"I telephoned him half an hour after the limousine left," Michael explained. "I told him that you were safe and I gave him directions to get here."

"He's supposed to come here, and should be arriving in a short while, my dear. But I wanted to talk to you first, to tell you why we've done this and to explain why I hadn't tried to contact you before."

Catherine looked at her mother—at the calm, almost regal manner she had—and her mind buzzed with unspoken questions.

"When Michael found me," Mrs. Moreau continued, "I had only been back in France for a few months. Before then I had occasionally come back to Paris to see you. At those times I would call Josephine to see if there was any chance of my catching a glimpse of you. She always arranged something so that I could see you without you seeing me. It was always painful for me, but joyful at the same time. I just couldn't give you up completely, you see."

"Why didn't you ever introduce yourself?" Catherine asked almost desperately.

"It would have caused more harm than good, " Edith said. "Your father would have made your life a misery, and you were entirely too young to understand what was going on. Then, when you were older, it just seemed wiser to leave things as they were. When I moved back to Paris, Josephine told me about you and Mathias, whom you must have suspected she doesn't like. At first I considered it your life and your decision . . . until recently. I saw a photo of you and Mathias in the paper and my heart almost stopped beating. You see, I recognized him. He isn't Mathias Brunton at all! His real name is Morris Burns, and he's wanted in Morocco for theft and drug trafficking."

"Mathias?" Catherine shook her head in bewilderment. It was all too incredible! She was having to assimilate too much in too short a time—her mother wasn't dead, Mathias wasn't who she thought he was . . . and here she was in some remote château, a kidnapped bride! Surely she had to be living in a nightmare!

"When I saw you with him in the newspaper photo, Catherine, I knew I would have to take action. I phoned your father at the office, but he hung up on me. After that I called repeatedly, but I could never get through to him again. I wrote letters that he never answered. Then one day a few weeks ago, I drove out to the factory and confronted him personally. I told him about Morris Burns, and said that if he didn't call off your marriage to that sordid character, I'd take drastic steps. He was livid and threatened to have me removed bodily from the premises. . . . It wasn't until later that I heard about his having had a heart attack that same day. At first I felt terribly guilty about it," she said, getting to her feet and gracefully crossing the oriental carpets to the fireplace.

"But in truth," she resumed, turning to face Michael and Catherine again, "he brought it on himself. If he had been straightforward with me eleven years ago, we might have worked things out between us, and at least saved our daughter some of her heartache if not our own. And if he had listened to me about Morris, none of what ensued would have occurred. I cannot believe for a moment, dear, that you're really in love with that man."

"Nor can I," Michael said. "I know you think I have an ulterior motive, Catherine, and to some extent, I do. But if this Burns would have made you happy, I never would have said anything against him—or even thought to check up on him, for that matter. After I met Edith, and she told me that he really wasn't Mathias Brunton . . . well, I spent a lot of late nights checking newspaper files and getting in touch with the authorities in Tangiers."

Strangely enough, Catherine was experiencing a kind of relief about what they were telling her. It was as if she'd been playing a role that didn't suit her, but one that she had felt compelled to continue with. For the first time in months she began to relax, and feel a little like her normal self. She realized with an inner shock that she had never really loved Mathias . . . that she had merely allowed herself to be swept up in his glamorous world. Between that and her father's urgings, she had almost got all the way to the altar. And in the nick of time she had been rescued from making what would have been a terrible mistake. "Go on," she said in a small voice.

"Mathias has a substantial police record, which includes arrest," Michael resumed. He was actually sent to prison in Tangiers eight years ago for involvement in narcotics."

"He escaped two years later, and was never heard from again," Mrs. Moreau added. "I remember following the coverage in the press. The police assumed he had fled either to South Africa or to the United States, but they had no leads. Oh, the usual notices were sent to authorities around the world, but I doubt that anyone made much of an attempt to actually find him. He wasn't a murderer or a terrorist, but just your run-of-the-mill crook."

"He still hasn't gone straight," Michael said, "That fancy sports can he drives and his expensive clothes are financed from his nefarious dealings. I believe we'll find, through a quick check, that Mathias Brunton has been taking kickbacks from clients of Moreau Electronics, and has probably been doing a bit of drug peddling, as well. We couldn't let you marry him, Catherine," he concluded firmly.

She took a deep breath and exhaled slowly, shaking her head. "I guess I owe you both a great deal. . . . And when father learns about Mathias, he's bound to be grateful, too."

"We'll soon find out," Edith said. "His car just pulled into the driveway."

Moments later the man in the blue sweater ushered Mr. Moreau into the room. "What's the meaning of this?" her father demanded. "Catherine! Are you all right?"

"Yes, father, I'm fine. Don't let yourself get upset,

please. Mother and Michael have done us both a tremendous service." How strange and sweet it felt to use the word "mother" about a living person.

"Come along, Catherine. You're coming home with me at once. I won't have you in the same room with that woman!"

"That woman," Edith said laconically, "happens to be this girl's mother and your legal wife, Pierre. And Catherine's not leaving here until you've heard us out."

Disgruntled, Pierre Moreau took a seat, tapping his fingers on his knees impatiently. "Well? Let's get this over with, Edith. Though why you think I would believe anything you say is beyond me."

Briefly, she repeated what they had already recounted about Mathias, and Michael confirmed the story with information he'd received from the Moroccan police as well as newspaper files.

"I can't believe it," Mr. Moreau said quietly at last.

"It's true," Edith said. "Michael has already contacted the authorities in Tangiers and they have arranged for extradition. The police should be arresting Mathias, or rather Morris, very soon now."

Pierre Moreau leaned forward and rested his head in his hands. "And to think I encouraged you to marry him," he mumbled wearily. "I almost ruined your life, Catherine," he said, looking up at her, "when all I wanted was your happiness and security."

"You had a head start on ruining her life eleven years ago, Pierre, and you've certainly done me no favors!" Edith's voice had a sharp stinging edge to it.

Michael moved over to the sofa where Catherine was sitting and took her hand in his. "I feel like an intruder," he whispered.

Catherine smiled wistfully. "You've earned the right to hear this," she murmured back. "And Michael, I have a lot of atoning to do. . . . I seem to have a great deal of my father in me. If I'd listened to you in the first place, well . . . ."

"You also have a lot of your mother in you," he said, squeezing her hand. "She's a fine woman, Catherine, and you can be proud of her."

"Don't take that tone with me, Edith, I won't have it!" Mr. Moreau was saying. "When you went away with Roberta and my brother for that weekend in the country, I adored you with all my heart and I trusted you."

"As well you should have!" Edith shot back.

"But when you didn't come back on Sunday, and Roberta said that you and Phillip were going to stay another night, I was confused and hurt. It was then that she told me you'd been carrying on with Phillip for months and that she could prove it."

"What? Are you mad?" Edith, who had begun to pace the room as if she were trying to work off her anger, stopped and faced her husband. "I always enjoyed Phillip's company, it's true. But we certainly never had an affair . . . or even thought of having one! What could have possibly made you believe her?"

With a bitter expression in his gray eyes, Mr. Moreau pulled out his wallet. "She gave me rather conclusive proof, which I carry with me always," he intoned, "lest I weaken and beg you to come back. You can read it for yourself, Edith."

She went over to him then and took the folded piece of paper, which she read and then handed to Catherine. "I clearly recall writing that note, Pierre. Why is this proof of anything?"

Catherine read the note quickly. *I won't be able to be with you tonight as planned. Don't worry, darling. Till tomorrow! All my love and kisses. Edith.*

"Roberta said she had found that note in Phillip's dresser drawer about a month previous to that weekend," Mr. Moreau said despondently. "I was sick with jealousy and enraged by your betrayal. I had to get you out of my house, out of my life, and away from our daughter before your deceit contaminated her, as well. Every time I saw our child after that, Edith, it was like a stab in my chest. She's always been the living image of you, tearing at my resolve to forget you entirely. I didn't dare love her too much, because I was afraid that she would turn out to be just like you. I couldn't have stood to have my heart broken twice!"

Quietly, slowly, Edith put her hand on her husband's shoulder. "Oh, Pierre, what fools we've been!" she said softly. "I asked Roberta to give you that note when she got back to St. Cloud so that you wouldn't worry. It was never intended for Phillip or for anyone but you."

"What . . . ?" His head came up, his gray eyes filled with the misery and pain he'd held in for so long. "You mean Roberta made up the whole thing? That all these agonizing years I've been living with a lie?"

"If only you had shown me this note then and had let me explain myself. . . . But no, you were too proud and arrogant." She turned away, her eyes glistening with tears that threatened to spill over. "Is that why you tried to seduce Roberta?"

"Seduce Roberta? What in heaven's name . . . . Oh, no! Did she tell you I tried to seduce her?"

The two of them stared at each other as the realization of what they had suffered needlessly hit them simultaneously.

"C'mon," Michael whispered to Catherine. "We should leave them alone now. They have a lot of talking to do."

He helped Catherine, encumbered as she was by her wedding dress, to her feet and, holding hands, they stole out of the room as quietly as they could. They crossed the huge entrance hall and entered another smaller salon. Michael closed the door behind them.

"It's hard to believe that they never gave each other a chance to explain what had happened," Catherine said solemnly, shaking her head.

"At least it's out in the open now," he replied. "I don't know if Edith will be able to forgive him, but the truth has been uncovered at long last."

"It's funny," Catherine said as they stood facing each other, "but you know my mother better than I do."

Michael smiled down at her. "It won't take you long to change that," he assured her. Then, gently pushing back her veil and cupping her chin in his hand, he asked, "Am I forgiven, Catherine?"

"Oh, Michael," she cried, unconscious that she was leaning toward him, "of course you are! I was being a spoiled, willful brat, that's all."

"A brat I happen to love very, very much," he said, bending down to kiss her.

His lips touched hers softly, then moved sensuously as he pulled her closer. Catherine's arms wound around his neck. As his kisses started sending little shivers throughout her body, she clung to him breathlessly, not caring at all that the ivory satin of her dress was being crushed against him.

It was a long while before Michael released her and looked down at her tenderly. "I suppose it's too soon to talk about it," he said, "but please remember that you mean everything to me, Catherine. I want you to marry me, but I also want you to be very sure that you love me first."

Aching to be in his arms again, she replied softly, "But how can you be so certain about me? Didn't you say you'd been in love twice before?"

He grinned at her. "Yes, and I meant it. I fell in love with you first when I was sixteen, and then all over again when I tumbled out of that tree and saw you bundled up on your terrace. Both times it was quite clear that you were the one for me. I was crazy about you—I always will be—and that's why I told you that being in love was like insanity."

"Insanity. . . . *I* was the crazy one, Michael, not to realize what I felt about you all along. I don't think it ever occurred to me why I always came to you whenever I needed advice or cheering up. I always felt so safe and warm and comforted when I was with you. I was blinded by the glitter of Mathias's world and I couldn't see where my true inclinations lay. I feel so foolish—and foolishly happy."

"I love you, Catherine," Michael replied, looking into her eyes.

"Hold me, Michael," she implored. "Please hold me always."

He pulled her toward him. "It's a deal," he said.

Mystique Books

Your Passport to High Adventure

LOVE
DANGER
INTRIGUE
ROMANCE
SUSPENSE
EXCITEMENT

Spellbinding stories
you won't be able to put down!

Look for

MYSTIQUE BOOKS

wherever paperback books are sold